Dimensions of Diasporic English Fiction

Dimensions of Diasporic English Fiction

Gauri Shankar Jha

GNOSIS

Nurturing the Aspirations

Worldwide Circulation through Authorspress Global Network

First Published 2011
by
GNOSIS

Editorial
Q-2A Hauz Khas Enclave,
New Delhi-110 016
e-mail: authorspress@yahoo.com

Marketing
E-35/103, Jawahar Park
Laxmi Nagar, Delhi-110 092
e-mail: authorspress@yahoo.com

An Imprint of Authorspress

Dimensions of Diasporic English Fiction
ISBN 978-93-81030-14-1

Printed in India at Tarun Offset, Delhi.

DEDICATED

TO

MY

GURUDEV

FAMILY

AND

FRIENDS

Acknowledgements

I am deeply indebted to the University Grants Commission (NERO), Guwahati, for sanctioning Grants-in-aid for undertaking the Minor Research Project on "Dimensions of Indian Diaspora Fiction" during Tenth Plan Period which enabled me to carry on such a valuable research work.

I am highly indebted to the publisher, Sudarshan Kcherry, who agreed, without condition, to publish the work immediately. Moreover, I cannot forget the help and cooperation that I got from my family members and friends to complete my work.

Gauri Shankar Jha

Preface

The present stature of Indian English literature is far away from its earlier image of being 'derivative' and 'imitative'. With its own 'independent' and 'distinct' identity it suffers from certain ambiguities. These writers, claiming to be Indian or included in the Indian English literature, have settled somewhere else, away from their homeland or prefer to be divorced from their ancestral being, and yet their works have an inclination towards their roots. Indian writers bracketed under expatriate/diaspora writers reflect certain exclusive trends that are altogether different from the major stay-at-home writers. Frankly speaking, the connotation of this word 'expatriation'/'diaspora' has undergone a sea-change with its expectation and reinterpretation as 'common phenomenon' all over the globe. There has been a distinct change in the psychological architecture of traditional man and modern man. It is a transition from a familiar frame of reference and relationship, and it is call for a reorientation of the entire social being. The reason attributed to such dramatic withdrawals and sensational callings are manifold such as the fleeing from political repressions, angst, loneliness, existential rootlessness, dissatisfaction or search for identity.

This study seeks to investigate/examine the aesthetic implications of expatriation for the fictional genre. Expressions of cultural, social and psychological centrality, that is, the creative focus of literary culture, has shifted to the margins damaging the perilous balance of literature. It is the outcome of the new literary situation created by deregionalised writers.

The technological evolution and dramatic different cultural situation have decreed that everyone is marginalised today. The multicultural situation has become a mode of perception. It is rampant in all literature of the world.

Dereliction is not a setback in the growth of an artist as he maintains constant touch with both his motherland and the present migrated world. As a result, Henry James, while writing for both Europe and America, never obliterates the memory of his 'imperfect' and 'incomplete' America; James Joyce tries to create a 'timeless myth, a universal mythology' but remains imprisoned in memories of Ireland; and T. S. Eliot confesses that his emotional roots lay in America alone. It happened with the Indian writers writing in English too. Most of the writers exhibit nostalgia, idealisation, inwardness, self-conscious intellectual writing, documentary realism in symbolic, allegorical and abstract modes, a pervasive dark vision in ironic and satiric writing, etc. Kamala Markandaya asserts her 'universals' rather than 'particular'; Ruth's realism is more 'abiding', and likewise. The influence of migration as the work on diaspora writers is visible in grappling for social identity, search for roots, compromising ego, etc. The writers grow allegorical, symbolic, cerebral, obscure, abstract and abstruse; their characters become typified and recondite, situations abstract and contrived, their language convoluted, obscure and private. They try to overcome the loss of ethos, culture and roots in different ways. They try to create authenticity, over-idealisation of nostalgia or satire, compatmentalisation, categorisation, etc. Here is a study that probes the Indian English Diasporic Fiction in its different perspectives.

Gauri Shankar Jha

Contents

1

The Diaspora Sensibility

In a sense, every one of us is Diasporic, that is, displaced from our original place and hankering for 'belonging'. Initially, this term 'Diaspora' was used for the Jews exiled from their homeland. Naturally, such a community has scattered and isolated existence, and has the ailing experience of cultural alienation and queer agony of being torn between two cultures, alien to each other, one abandoned and the other adopted. Precisely, this is the phenomenon of people's displacement.

In the seventeenth century came the colonialism and such displacements got impetus whereas in the eighteenth and nineteenth centuries the process uprooted people from their native places to serve the British Empire in different parts of the world. A strong nostalgia for the 'roots', a yearning for the 'home', an acute sense of isolation, an agony of unbelonging and uprootedness, pains of being marginalised and insecurity, identity crisis, cultural conflict, dissemination and above all, the state of *Trishanku* are some of the distinguishing features of this community. They have to suffer oppressions of different sorts: political, economic, religious, etc. They are the 'other' in the new land. The Diasporas occupy diverse space and so all of them cannot be clubbed together, though they have a common sense of being in exile and they share the same sensibility as per their perception, attitude and concern—that of, displacement, rootlessness, discrimination, marginalisation, identity crisis, cultural conflict, etc. It is not that the narration of Diasporic story is only its negative proposition, rather it has its positive stand also, and that is the growth and transformation in the subjectivities, and facilitates cultural interaction, opening new routes in the fast changing socio-cultural, economic and political global scenario, enhancing the output of their creativity and endeavour. It is the expatriate sensibility, the direct consequence of cultural disparity and emotional integration. There is the basic difference between expatriation and immigration in respect of assimilation; an expatriate carries his home/country with him, as we find with V. S. Naipaul and Bharati Mukherjee, dealing with Indian life realistically and poignantly which at times appear to be ironical.

In an alien land such people are recognised in great dismay in their isolation, and the uncertain hazards and perilous risks of the new land. The compulsions forced them to live in crowded tenements, breeding associations of different sorts, uniting them with common understanding, sympathy and cooperation. Such associations acquired financial stability and spread their tentacles in different directions. So the agony persists; characters are caught between two cultures and life becomes horrible: as treasure of "agonised inspiration, multiple identities, new subjectivities, creative memoirs and fresh perspectives on language and life", though 'there has been a tremendous quantitive and qualitative change in the phenomenon of Diaspora owing to the great demographic upheavals of the last century, especially, its last decades'(Satchidananan, 2003, 50).

It is also presumed that these people remain in cultural solitude and as Homi Bhabha points out in *Location of Culture* (Bhabha,1994), a hybrid location of antagonism, perpetual tension and pregnant chaos. Sura P. Rath calls it "*Trishanku*" in his article, "Home(s) Abroad: 'Diasporic Identities in Third Spaces'" (*Journal of Contemporary Thoughts,* M. S. University, Baroda, Summer, 1999).

It has been also said that "the products of this hybrid locations are results of a long history of confrontations between unequal cultures and forces, in which the stronger cultures to control, remake, or eliminate the subordinate partner" (Lavie, Smadar and Swedenburg, Ted, ed., *'Displacement, Diaspora, and the Geographies of the Identity,* Duke Univ. Press, Durham, 1996).

According to Bhabha:

> The negotiation of cultural identity involves the continual interface and exchange of cultural performances that is in turn produce a mutual recognition (or representation) of cultural difference. The social articulation of difference from the minority perspective is a complex on-going negotiation that seeks to authorise cultural hybrities that emerge in moments of historical transformation. (Satchidanand, 2003, 52)

Here Bhabha finds individual and local experiences of Diasporic writers as a part of the larger process of historical change, the inter-subjective and collective experiences of nation, community interest or cultural values are negotiated in the emergence of the intricacies, the overlap and displacement of domains of difference. Such representation is not to be hastily read as the reflection of pre-given ethnic or cultural traits set in the fixed tablet of tradition taken together.

The Diasporic experience is influenced by the context of immigration, and so we find the difference between the neo-colonial and post-colonial Diasporic experience. The earliest phase was that of forced immigration, for instance, trying to escape the religious and other political or social persecution. Later on, the purpose was changed; it was in search of a better life, prosperity and material success. On the other hand, we find many academics and war-time labourers whom Prof. Satchidanand calls 'resident aliens' because of their intact 'home and identity' back to their native places. The most noticeable things were that of class, language and gender which surfaced paradoxically, including minority–majority status. Among the women Diasporic creative writers we have Meena Alexander, Panna Naik, Malati Rao, Sudha Chandola, Sujata Bhatt, Anita Desai, Kamala Markandaya, Bharati Mukherjee, Suniti Namjoshi, Jhumpa Lahiri, etc.

These Diasoporic populations create diverse impression in the land where they reside, for instance, a Tamil in Sri Lanka or an Indian in Mauritius is taken to be a threat because of the size of their population. In the same way the question of a second generation or third generation migrant is also different from the first generation; for them the image of homeland is completely different: they reconstruct their homeland from the fragments of information gathered from hearsay, from the interest or from other sources which are not authentic at all. These people do not want to go back to their homeland, rather opt to fantasise about and sometimes prefer to visit as a tourist or guest for a few days to gather superficial information. Obviously, there is diversity in the experience of struggle for identity, belongingness or otherness. The most dominating experience is that of 'otherness' which may not be a crippling experience, but it is a time that tells us to redefine one's 'self', to ascertain one's identity which includes the place of belonging, past and present, the context of time as history and myth. Prof Satchidanand is of the view that "Post-colonialism seems to come full circle in those writers who inhabit in the third space, live the third culture and shape the third history."

We may have colonial-indological concept of India derived from nationalistic discourse and leading to federal democratic perspective of a polyphonic India which is the direct consequence of a mosaic of cultures, languages and literatures, with a worldwide of the essentials, particularly of the Orientals. However, Diasporic writers' perception of eternal India contrary to the Indian writers (whom we may call as the writers-at-home) concentrates on alternative nationhood, different imagined communities, etc. Homi Bhabha believes that the wandering peoples of the Diaspora mark a shifting boundary that alienates the frontiers of the modern nation. It appears to be interruption of the monologist discourse of modern metropolises with their imperial memories of the disinherited unsettling imperial inheritance challenging the monolith of modern Western nation, fostering cultural nationalism by suggesting Hindu hegemony. Diasporic ideologies believe in reproducing patriarchy, class structure and ethnic conflicts too; in some cases practising apartheid is also found in the Diasporic community more than that we find in the Western racial discrimination. Most of the Diasporic writers are aware of the inherent contradictions, multiple possibilities of alienation and assimilation, retreat into the old set patterns and revolt against them, of being the coloniser and the colonised, marginal and central, including the social structure (based on class and sect distinction), family structure (based on patriarchal norms, etc.) and the sense of roots (based on the concept of home, belongingness, etc.). The concept of unisonant nation with a single unified culture has become obsolete now; the concept of Diaspora based on linguistic and regional– cultural terms in vogue today. We Indians have a cosmopolitan character and multi-cultural milieu, and have the experience of an alienation, a solitude, a torment of the absurd and the irrational and an existential angst as intense and as creative as that of, say, Kafka, Beckett, Sartre or Albert Camus—exquisite in their distrust in the system, fear of the crowd, the experience of boredom, philosophic detachment, fragmentariness of expression and nostalgia for the old home.

Jana Evans Braziel in his book *Diaspora: An Introduction* defines Diaspora as "a term historically and typically the scattering of people in their homelands into new communities across the globe" (24). He further quotes William Safram *(Diaspora in Modern Societies: Myths of Homeland and Return)* defining the term Diaspora (in contrast with other related but distinct categories: expatriates, immigrants, refugees, aliens) as characterized by six distinguishing characters/features:

> First, diaspora as a term refers to people who have been dispersed from a specific original 'center' to two or more 'peripheral', or foreign regions; second, diaspora applies when those dispersed communities "retain a collective memory, vision, or myth about their original homeland—its physical location, history and achievements"; third, Diasporic communities are marked by a firm belief that "they are not—and perhaps cannot be—fully accepted by their host society and therefore feel partly alienated and insulated from it"; fourth, diasporas overwhelmingly "regard their ancestral homeland as their true, ideal home and as the place to which they or their descendants would (or should) eventually return—when conditions are appropriate"; fifth, Diasporic communities firmly "believe that they should collectively, be committed to the maintenance or restoration of their original homeland and to its safety and prosperity"; and sixth, diaspora and diasporic communities typically "relate, personally or

> vicariously, to that homeland in one way or another, and their ethno-communal consciousness and solidarity are importantly defined by the existence of such relationship." (24-25)

Another critic Robin Cohe (in *Global Diasporas*) adds to this definition of Diaspora as "groups that scatter for aggressive or voluntarist purposes" including revolutionary minorities struggling for an imaginary homeland as well as those travelling for commercial trade; secondly Diasporic consciousness taken as "strong tie to the past or a block to assimilation in the present and future;" thirdly, Diasporas or Diasporic consciousness defined positively as "recognition of the positive virtues of retaining a Diasporic identity, that is, often a creative, enriching one;" fourthly, "members of Diaspora characteristically sense not only a collective identity in a place of settlement, nor again only relationship with an imagined, putative or real homeland, but also some common identity with co-ethnic members in other countries." (25)

Within the contemporary critical moments of post-colonialism, post-modernity, and late capital of possibility of articulation of Diaspora (as a term) and gained new ground and are being circulated as 'new currencies' in global discourses with parameters of geography, 'national identity and belongingness —with geopolitical, material, technological, environmental, human and cultural terrains, challenging strictures and structures of nationalism and the increasingly imperialist, hegemonic forces of globalization.

Obviously, Diaspora emerge as 'double pronged critique, of the nation and globalization. Brazil is of the opinion that Diasporas are transnational 'tentacles' of nation–states, both those of the homeland and of the country of adoption, but Diasporas are also "global capitalist economic formation created by push/pull factors within national economics, regional trading blocs and even within the production and labour shifts of the global economy"(26). It is very surprising that the term Diaspora is also used as synonymous of 'transnationalism' and 'global capitalism', though it remains "a primarily human form of movement across geographical, historical, linguistic, cultural and national boundaries." We need to understand the migratory pattern in order to understand Diaspora as a theoretical, sociological, anthropological, historical, and cultural and geographical term. John Decker in his book, *1492, The Politics of Diaspora*, defines Diaspora as:

> By diaspora, minimally defined, I mean a sense of belonging to move then one history, to move than one time and place, more than one past and future. Diaspora suggests belonging to both the omnipresent weight of pain of being an outsider in a new one. Diaspora suggests both lack and excess of loss and separation, yet also the possibility of new adventures of identity and the continued imagining of unconquerable countries of the mind.(VII- VIII)

In the post-modern world of the multiple, fragmented, contradictory identities that question of one's own identity, it becomes paradoxical, embarrassing, contemptible and inauthentic, as discussed in Edward Said's 'Orientalism" which discusses colonialism, post-colonialism, migration, Diaspora, exile, belonging, identity, ethnicity and race.

A.L. Mcleod opines in his book *The Literature of Indian Diaspora*:

> The term diaspora, from the Greek, meaning dispersal, distribution, or spreading, has been applied for many years to the world wide scattering of the Jews; in more recent times it has been applied to a number of ethnic and racial groups living distant from their traditional homelands; and it has been used with particular application to people from the former British India. (IX)

Normally, Indian Diaspora means writers of Indian birth or ethnicity living abroad, who may be first generation expatriate whose India was home—of nourishment, values, inclination, love and affection though it may not be a universal case, with distinct dissonance. In the same way, the literature of the Indian Diaspora is "that body of writing in English produced by persons who identify themselves as of Indian heritage who are living (or have lived for some time) outside Mother India in such places as Fuji, Trinidad and Guyana (where they are substantial minorities and may shortly become majorities) and in Mauritius, Malaysia, and East Africa, or in Western countries such as Australia, Canada, United States, and Britain" (X). Such writings are available not just in general prose and poetry but in more esoteric genres of drama, oratory, philosophy, theology, literary history and criticism. Dr. Graham Huggan feels that "a consolidation of Diaspora into trendy theories of hybridity, nomadic, and borderlands, served as a comforting substitute for genuine social activities was evidently one that many others shared, and any writer seen to operate in such a way came in for sharp criticism, one suspects as a displacement of private concerns." Huggan cites the instance of Naipaul to show how displacements of inner drives and fears can operate and the element of inherent imperialism in travelogues, though the Diasporic subjects are often treated as hybrid, interstitial, tactically mobile, and asserting an integrated selfhood specifically located and having clear social agency.

For human beings migration and dispersion are natural phenomenon which may be categorised as temporary, seasoned or permanent migration from their original habitat for various reasons. N. Jayram is of the view that migration does not mean physical movement of people only rather migrants carry with them a socio-cultural baggage which among other things consists of:

a) A predefined social identity

b) A set of religious belief s and practices

c) A framework of norms and values governing family and kinship organisation, and food habits, and,

d) Language (16)

These migrants keep in touch with their homeland, called 'the myth of return', their identities are twofold—that of the homeland and that of the land of adoption, that is, originating from and belonging to; it further helps in formation ethnicity, different ethnic group and likewise.

Going by etymology, the term Diaspora is derived from the Greek composite verb 'dia' and, speirein' (infinitive), literally meaning, 'to scatter', 'to spread', or to 'disperse'. It was originally used to refer to the dispersion of Jews after the Babylonian exile in 586 BC and to the aggregate of Jews or Jewish communities scattered in exile outside Palestine. In current parlance, however, the term is applied to describe any group of people who are so dispersed and so are the people of Indian subcontinent.

Ours is a distinct Diasporic entity with unique socio-cultural history used to different economic and political situation, reflecting varying degrees of survival, persistence or retention of several social patterns and cultural elements thoroughly Indian, to enliven them and to revive them, as a kind of Renaissance of Indian culture. With the same ethnic identity they negotiate with multicultural societies of the alien land, with active economic and cultural competitions, experiencing ethnic discrimination either explicit or convert, including the academic operations too.

The imagination of India has a long history and can be divided into three groups for convenience of study and knowledge, that is, Indian Diaspora in

a) Pre-colonial period

b) Colonial period

c) Post-colonial period

In our survey of history of ancient India we find the instances of Buddhist *bhikhus* travelling to remote corners of central and Easatern India, contact between kingdoms of Coromandel coast and islands of South-east Asia, contact of the Places of Bengal with the Sailendra kings of Indonesia, the expeditions of the South Indian Cholas, evidences of Hindu and Buddhist religion, mythology and culture in the South-east Asia (Thailand and Bali), trade with East Africa and permanent settlement there, colony of Indian merchants ay Memphis and Egypt in 500 BC, etc.

Indian Diaspora during European colonialism is a crucial phase in Indian Diaspora. It was by the first quarter of the nineteenth century that demand for labour force accounted and opposition to slavery and eventual abolition intensified; three distinct patterns evolved: 'indentured' labour emigration, 'kangani' and 'maisty' labour emigration, and 'passage' or 'free' emigration.

Indian Diaspora in the post-colonial period is also a significant phase in which three distinct patterns can be identified: the emigration of Anglo-Indian to Australia and England, the emigration of professionals and semi-professionals to the industrially advanced countries (like USA, England and Canada), and the emigration of skilled and unskilled labourers to West Asia.

The study of Indian Diaspora is complex and variegated and cannot be bracketed under any exclusive or conventional discipline. As per its theoretical and conceptual apparatuses, it is essentially multi disciplinary in nature. The causes and condition for migration may be broadly categorised as the push forces and pull factors, voluntary or involuntary, due to prevalent economic, political and social condition. If we go by the historical accounts, we find that the emigrants from India have been heterogeneous lot, varied in regional, religious, caste, occupational, linguistic and cultural backgrounds. The most interesting aspect is the socio-cultural baggage carried by the first generation emigrants from India, that of religion, language, music, art, dress, cooking, etc., with regional variants, some of these elements have disappeared, some survived and some assimilated syncretised or changed whereas some revived. In multiethnic politics and in places of dominating Indian population, the question of images and identity has been critical: in the colonial phase the image was that of 'coolies'; in literature we find such expressions as 'East Indians', 'Girmitiyas', 'the Asians' and the prefix 'Indo'. The issue of ethnicity gets politicised and lead to struggle for political power and the subsequent violent conflicts, exodus of Indian community, etc. William Safran in his book *Diaspora in Modern Societies: Myths of Homeland and Return*, says:

> They (the immigrants) continue to relate personally or vicariously, to the homeland in one way or another, and their ethno-communal consciousness and solidarity are importantly defined by existence of such a relationship. (84)

Irrespective of disciplinary orientation, two theoretical frameworks have been adopted in the analysis of this community: the socio-cultural perspective and political economy perspective. The socio-cultural perspective focuses on cultural identity and integration of the Diasporic communities, operating within the parameters of conventional structural-functionalism, addressing the questions of socio-cultural continuity and change within it, taking into consideration their dynamics in context of multiculturalism. On the other hand, political economy perspective focuses on the socio-economic thinking of the non-Marxist, the Marxist and neo-Marxists. This immigrant population work as social laboratories for the study and testing certain key social processes like the formation of ethnic identity, shaping of ethnic relations, the reconstruction of institutions, the reconstruction of life-worlds, etc. ; it also provides unique avenues for understanding the dynamics of culture. The first generation of immigrants was keen to avoid conflicts with the host society. This lot was not a homogeneous social and cultural group. Their system of adjustment was that of 'accommodationists' or 'integrationists'. It is expected that there should be 'an eventual unification of discourse' for a better understanding between the two cultures.

'Home' has been defined by Sushila Nasta in her book *Home Truths* as:

> . . . not necessarily whereon starts from. In the post-colonial literary studies, the question of 'home' has increasingly come to be vexed terrain. This is not surprising. For the notion of 'home', with all the political, ideological and symbolic baggage that it still implies, was one which formed an integral part of the naturalized rhetoric of Britain as Europe and has lingered on in the nationalistic grammar of Britain as post-imperial nation. . . . The seductive power of 'home', both as a force for authority over and as a continuing domestic metaphor for maintaining a means of authority within, figures most forcefully." (1)

In a Diasporic space we grow with new identities and subjectivities with new alliances. Diaspora desire is for a lost homeland. While talking of Indian Diaspora fiction in English, so many questions pop up in our mind, for instance, does it have its independent identity, does it possess some unique characteristics that determine its separate status, does it reflect 'Indianness' in true sense, how such writers rule over Indian English writing and so on and so forth. Such writings that appear to me a maze of nothingness repeating the same sort of ideas in every piece of writing, in almost all works of all writers; you may call it a negative procreation, yet my exoneration lies in the following proposition; for this purpose I would like to select a few writers only and their works, for the simple reason that this brief paper cannot cover its wide horizon.

Normally Diaspora fiction lingers over alienation, loneliness, homelessness, existential rootlessness, nostalgia, questioning, protest and assertions and quest of identity; it also addresses issues related to amalgamation or disintegration of cultures. Discrimination, margins of two different social milieus, internalizing nostalgia and suffering a forced amnesia—we may call it a literary/cultural phenomenon with a distinct melting pot syndrome or that of *Salad bowl* where identity of each ingredient is under question. Surprisingly, the writer has to relocate himself afresh, for which he has to undergo penance such as readjustment, adaptation, participation and fulfilment amidst dilemmas and self-imposed *ghettoisation.* But what about the Nobel Laureate V.S. Naipaul, my first target. Where does he stand now? He associates himself with one stance the next moment he deviates; his selection for the Nobel prize is under question—is it for his old-fashioned travelogues, or for his autobiographical novels, or his inconsistent stories or his deciduous articles. He does not possess anything uncommon and so he cannot be taken on par with Raja Rao, Mulk Raj Anand or Shri Aurobindo, the pillars of Indian English writing. Let us analyze his work first. To his credit, we find a plethora of works: in the name of novels *The Mystic Masseur, The Suffrage of Elvira, Miguel Street, A House for Mr. Biswas, Mr. Stone and The Knights Companion, The Mimic Men, In a Free State, Guerrillas, A Bend in the River, Half a Life,* etc.; in the name of travelogues, *The Middle Passage, An Area of Darkness, India:*

a Wounded Civilization, etc. in the name of short stories, his two books *A Flag on the Island* and *The Loss of EIdorado,* and in the name of collection of articles we have *The Overcrowded Barracoon.* Movingly his house is overcrowded as he is a full timer writer and, in this regard, his dedication cannot be questioned. *The Mystic Masseur* (1957), *The Suffrage of Elvira* (1958) *and Miguel Street* (1959) deal with the rootlessness of Trinidadian society who resort to adoption, compromise, submission, etc. for sheer survival. *An Area of Darkness* has frustration and disappointment out of nostalgia for the old land. *A House for Mr. Biswas* is concerned with homelessness, as John Thieme explains:

> A complete portrait of Hindu life in colonial Trinidad has been realized through the description of Mr. Biswas' experiences in each of the novel's many hours which represent: the passive dependent life of the child; the Hindu's dependent states as a member of the extended family; as abortive attempt an escape through small time capitalism (the chase); the construction of plantation system(the Barraqcks); the impossibility of complete emancipation (the house he builds at green vale and near short hills); unsuccessful parody of phantocracy (Short hills) and finally, the partial freedom possible, once one has realized one's limitations (the St. James House). (Thieme, 1915, 12)

Here my contention is whether Trinidadian Hindu society is a real Hindu / Indian society on the basis of which Naipaul draws the whole picture and tries to justify his stand. Not only that, such misleading projections invites erroneous reactions and criticism, too, from what India or Indian society is. Again, search for house is not only related to Diaspora life rather it is a common characteristic of the present life, it is a global weakness. On the other hand, Naipaul's assertions of his perfect knowledge of India—its civilization and culture—of Hindu society and even Muslim culture does not appear to be sound enough to be relied. We do not have any evidence whether he has gone through our ancient scriptures like Eliot and Yeats, but, certainty he pretends to be so, and voice against capitalism is the fashion of the day. Besides, it has autobiographical reflections too. The point that I wish to emphasize is that Naipaul does not possess anything that we may call innovative or novel, and such Diasporic writing is totally irrelevant. Naiplul's making may be different, as K. Shivarama Karanth puts it:

> Rights and wrongs, dangers and rewards and many similar elements force an individual to avoid or choose courses of action...creative literature is not a marathon race. If experiences are our urge to writing, how do we evaluate such experiences? Life consists of so many things that make it a whole. Which part or aspect is important? There are so many individual elements and the totality is life . . . (Karanth, 1990, 8-24)

Naipaul's life seems to be betraying totality and his works are consciously carved out insufficient patterns. It is not an ideologically innocent gesture, rather a conscious exercise revealing conflicts, repressions and contradiction suffered at the personal level. In this context Homi Bhabha seems to be more relevant as he says:

> The very idea of pure ethnically cleared national identity can only be achieved through the death, literal and figurative, of the complex inter-weaving of history and the culturally contingent borderlines of modem nationhood. (Bhabha, 1994, 5)

Naipaul is in almost abnormal obsession with the idea of India, gets disenchanted when confronted with the ground reality and in all his texts keeps on hovering. The same thing happens with Rushdie's egocentric Salim Sinai in 1981 and Professor Malik Solanka in 2001, as the 'wounded self", 'energetic fury', 'lightening strings of puppet' and 'helpless nonviolent'. Similar is the case of Vikram Seth, Amit Chaudhari, Rohinton Mistry and others. Graham Huggan explains it more clearly, Mediated events (refers to the Barcelona Conference 'India: Fifty Years After', in Sept. 1997) such as these are characteristic of the current appeal of India- and more specifically of Indian Literature in English consumer item"(Huggan, 2001,59). However, Huggan has to accept such trend as specific to Diaspora writing as he further suggests:

> The future of Indian literature in English at the millennium seems indisputable, the reputations of its best known writers intact, its commercial success virtually ensured. Yet it remains a cause for concern that nearly all the recognized writers are located in the Diaspora. (Huggan, 2001,17-78)

Not only that Diaspora writing displays its post-modern trait, too, as pointed out by Linda Hutcheon:

> Post-modernism has art forms that are fundamentally self-reflexive, in the other words, art that is self consciously art (on artifice), literature that is openly aware of the fact that it is written and read as part of a particular culture, having as much to do with the literary past as with the social present. (Hutcheon, 1988, 12)

In fact, it is not subversion of true issue, nor a staggering exercise rather deep concern and anguish the lost identity of the land of exile, in search of (perhaps) some cosmetic remedies. It is the ability to conceive India from outside with premature nationalist sentiments and its rich culture with myopic eyes but never India, as it is. The reader is left awestruck: is it an appeal to racial purity, militarism, violence and religious orthodoxy— taking nation as an emotional, spiritual, religious, catholic and missionary identification of a people—a new species with hybrid identities: racial, ethnic, regional and national; the writing fall within the domain of exile, trial and homecoming. Naiplul and other Diaspora writers appear to be handicap, as they do not have a tradition of their own, it maybe the particular social, political, philosophical structure of the existing society of England or America or Canada or any other country, consequently their work remain without a meaningful hero—perhaps a multiracial immigrant, slave (of imposed culture or colonial compulsions) restless to establish their identity; this anguishing experience of a lack of tradition remains the hallmark of their fiction. Not surprisingly, their search becomes trap as the form/theme they adopt prove to be repetitive of the colonial drive or otherwise; the man here is without a core, running after a mirage with an intense desire to live in the present, with unanswerable future and strong pull of the past/the root, as Nietzsche puts it, in *Thus Spoke Zarathustra*: "In each Now, Being begins; round each Here turns the sphere of There. The centre is everywhere. But is the path of eternity:"(Marcuse, 1956,122) Salman Rushdie is right in his observation when he says:

> In the modem age we have come to understand our own selves as composites, often contradictory, even internally incompatible, we have understood that each of us is many different people. Our younger selves differ from our older salves; we can be bold in the company of our employers, principled when we instruct our children and corrupt when offered some secret temptation; we are serious and frivolous, loud and quiet, aggressive and easily abashed. The nineteenth century concept of the integrated self has been replaced by this jostling crowd of I's. And yet unless we are damaged or deranged, we usually have a relatively clear sense with my many selves to call all of them 'me'. (*The Observer*, 10 August. 1997)

Naipaul intends to identify himself with the prevalent reality: social, political or personal, yet his world suffers from certain constraints such as lack of enterprising nationality, despair and anguish, undefined social potential, imperfect empathy, orchestration of perceptions, multiple, metaphorical implications paradox of ceremonial departures, danger of non-existence and the compulsion to adopt the same beaten path. Consequently *The Enigma of Arrival* introduces a changed man, disillusioned on arrival at the land of his imagination; *In a Free State* projects a biased protagonist, victim of alienation, loneliness and despair; *Guerrillas* laments the social situation: thoroughly materialistic, without faith, ideas or ideals, exhausted in all ways, "about the unity of experience and the illusion of pain" (261); *A Bend in the River* presents the structural and psychological balance between the subjective and objective, internal and external, 'I' and 'We" society and individual colonial West and colonized Third World, ideas and actuality; *Mr. Stone and the Knight's Companion* humanizes its narrator Mr. Stone; *A House for Mr. Biswas* cites an a orphan 'Mr. Biswas' maligned by the sense of excessive insecurity coupled with an urge of freedom, self imprisoned egoist, subjective, personal and unfit; *The Mystic Masseur* aspires for power; *The Suffrage of Elvira* necessitates the political awakening; *The Mimic Men* questions the coexistences of politics and simplicity; and *Half a Life,* precisely, delineates an autobiography of Diaspora self. Finally, Naipaul admits in his reception speech to the Nobel Committee and the Swedish Academy at Stockholm on 7 Dee. 2001, "I am the sum of my books". Naipaul's writing confirms Paranjape's observation:

> Since Diaspora writing emanates from identity formation leading to further and more sophisticated articulation of identity) or manifest in community national hood, and also huge global contexts it is important to remember and perceive Diaspora space as at all time explanatory, fluid and dynamic so that intersections within histories, past and futures do not congeal into rigid boundary laden states. (Paranjape, 2001, 59)

Perhaps, it is a typical twentieth century literary phenomenon, as pointed out in *Selected Writing of Gertrude Stein:* "'So the twentieth century is . . . a time when everything cracks, where everything is destroyed, everything isolates itself; it is a more splendid thing then a period where everything follows itself." Bharati Mukherjee, too, can be bracketed under the same category, though she considers herself an American and claims to have overthrown "the smothering tyranny of nostalgia and surmounted the temptation of *ghettoization*" (Mukherjee, 1992, 35) contrary to her assertion, the cultural references and the inter-texts that she uses in her writing defies her own statement establishing something else: available in her handling of the theme of individuality, 'outsider/insider', 'otherness', Indians customs, patriarchal tradition and shift to American paradigms such as individual expression, autonomy and the pursuit of happiness very distinct in the progression of her writing the early and the later one's. Her journey from *The Tiger's Daughter* (1971) to *Desirable Daughter* (2001) exhibits her movement away from the 'aloofness of expatriation' to the 'exuberance of immigration' (Darkness, 3); Naipaul is her mentor; she confesses:

> In myself I detect a pale and immature reflection of Naipaul; it is he who has written most movingly about the pain and absurdity of art and exile of 'third world art' and exile among the former colonizers; the tolerant incomprehension of hosts, the absolute impossibility of ever having a home, a 'Desh'. (Clark & Mukherjee, 1977, 287)

Her 'Tara' of *The Tiger's Daughter* is a typical product of Indian society, a victim of Indianness, fails to cope with the American cultural milieu, suffers from the sense of insecurity and instability, and finds herself nowhere; she is very much like Naipaul's Mr. Biswas, O'Neill's Mr. Yank and most of the characters of the twentieth century Diaspora writing, in search of identity, dignity, belongingness and a place of one's own; it may be construed as a satirical picture of an Indian women who resorts to the protection of her father or a father like figure on husband whenever confronted with crisis, obviously passive and dependent, in firm grip of fear and alienation like Dimple of, *Wife*. Dimple's obsession is 'Americanization'; and so she prefers to obliterate her past roots and finally disillusioned, her fantasy world shattered, leading to the killing of her husband as an act of self assertion; this is the tragic journey of an Indian wife initiating her journey from the model of Sita and culmination in the so-called American progressive society of infidelity, pregnancy, abortion, murder and blackmail; this is a typical theme of Diasporic fiction, often called East. West encounter, a psychic-social problem on psycho-analytical approach of expatriate writing. Jasmine's protagonist, too, has the same fate. Analogy with Naipaul is evident as she admits in *Dankness*: "Like Naipaul, in whom I imagined a model, I tried to explore state-of-the-art expatriates. Like Naipaul, I used a mordant and self protective irony in describing my character's pain" (2).

Another writer who deserves to be cited is Prof. Satendra Nandan who is a Fijian-Indian or Indian Australian having commitment to respect the condition of the Fijian-Indians in his poems and prose pieces such as *Line Across Black Water* (Poems), *Voice in the River* (Poems), *Faces in a Village* (poem), *The Wounded Sea* (Novel) and *Requiem for Rainbow*; once again, Naipaul is a great influence here and so the same theme of nostalgia, displacement and dilemmas, survival and progress, under the hostile sky, pluralistic and symbiotic co-existence of the major ethnic communities harrowing reality of multiculturalists nations (as Fiji) fragmented and fragmentary selves, ethnic hatred and discrimination, exile and dispossession, peripatetic and multilayered existence, lost homelands and the travails of arriving and departures, belongings and alienations, imaginary homelands and creative continuum, poignancy and pain. aesthetic and political, abduction and confinement, civilized and civilizing world, cultural and spiritual awakening, etc. also true for Meena Abdullah and Christopher Cyrill in *The Time of the Peacock* (1965) and *The Ganga and its Tributaries* (1993). Coming to *Requiem for a Rainbow* of Prof. Nandan, we can very easily trace the autobiographical touches, and he admits, about his writing:

> . . . like my life it is flawed and fragmentary. But it is a story, or a version of it one's life is, in the final analysis, the ultimate text. It would be pretentious to call it a memoir; it is certainly a piece of autobiographical writing. . . . This is one ordinary son's extraordinary experience. (Preface, 12)

It is a story of the marginalized and dispossessed as Naipaul's mimic men: "We were the mimic men so compellingly and lethally explored in Vidia Naipaul's novel of the same name. Be had delineated. without sentimentality or compromise, the malaise of our lives" (45). The first two chapters *Fourteenth May: an Eclipse* and *Suva: the Twice Banished* have the history of a failed nation-state whereas *Nadi: The River Between, Delhi: A Light Among the Ruins* and *Canberra: The Golden Grove Unleaving* have Diaspora consciousness coping with the inevitable process of displacement and replacement, true story of thousand of Fijian Indians, going back to the past, in search of their roots) identity and belongingness. "Like India, it's for me a deeply beautiful world, but difficult to live up to its meaning for an individual" (71). The Diaspora self is the eternal wanderer, away from the paradise, their home: "Most of our people have become homeless in their own home country, strangers among familiar faces, lived spaces. They say exiles live in one place and remember the reality of another; one belongs where one cannot be, and one is where one does not belong" (Pre.11). Prof. Nandan and Naipaul have the same things to say as a common approach of Diaspora fiction.

Christopher Cyrill's *The Ganga and its Tributaries* carry the same massage: "I once wanted you to marry an Indian girl, but now I want you to mix your genes. You are an Anglo Indian born in Australia. You are like a Trinity Marry mix. . ." (146). In Cyril's *The Ganga and it's Tributaries* the Australian born boy dreams of places in India made known to him by his parents; in his day-dreams and thoughts the landscapes are interchangeable: "It occurred to me one day as I watched the model that India had roughly the same outline a Australia" (21), and again, "My uncle and aunt spoke with accents that reminded me of the accents of the men who set on an nature strip and my father was also talking with an accent" (28). Cyrill has deliberately marginalized the white Australian figure in his work; the canvas is filled with India and Indians only; his friend Jack finds himself displaced; but the solidarity of his own family remains intact In Mena Abdullah's *The Time of the Peacocks*, Indian food and Punjabi accent (Indian English) dominates and Cyrill's characters who have the same Indian English used in the family. Indian awareness is evident in the conversation:

> There is the soul of Brahmin in thee. Thou knowest how to flatter and please. Thou knowest the words that should be true. (Abdullah, 1973, 39).

Though living in distant land these writers cannot divorce their relationship with their earlier social milieus. Edward Said explains it as a man made historical progress:

> . . . Men make their own history, that what they can know is what they have made, and extend it to geography: as both geographical and cultural entities to say nothing of historical entities, such locals, regions, geographical sectors as 'Orient' and 'Occident' are manmade. Therefore as much as the West itself, the Orient is an idea that has a history and a tradition of thought, imagery and vocabulary that have given it reality and presence in and for the West. The two geographical entities thus support and to an extent reflect each other. (Said, 1978, 5)

This particular action can be explained with Jung's concept too, "The conscious mind is based upon and result from as unconscious psyche which is prior to consciousness and continues to function together with or despite consciousnesses" (Jung, 1940, 13). My focus, precisely, is on a common ground where different cultures meet, interact, resist and reconcile; such reconciliation does not ignore resistance, rather it is a prerequisite; it is here in Diasporic function that cultures come in contact with each other, they affirm and deny each other, accepts and discards, acknowledges and resists, selects and rejects, and the ambivalence continues endlessly. We may notice in Bharati Mukherkjee in India (or in the Bengali Indian ghetto in Now York) and gradually hybridization starts, Americanization creeps in and cultural indicators have no distinct mark, it becomes 'Christian-Hindu-Muslim' self or 'American-English-Indian' self on likewise, and Bharati Mukherjee makes it clear in her interview with Tirthankar Chanda in 1996:

> I wrote *The Tiger's Daughter* when I was a real expatriate. I thought of beginning, middle and end from an omniscient, god-like point of view. I was also ionizing the traditional Anglo Indian Fiction, but I still thought of the cosmos like I whole entity and I could step aside and look on the characters as fitting in a certain perspective. By the time. I came to write *'Wife'* which came out in 1975, I could introduce a limited third person who would not have the gods in his/ her toes. I was standing just behind the shoulder of one character *'Wife'* has got a lot more bitterness, more venom, and more energy"(*Commonwealth*, vol.18, No.2, p.56).

We notice the transformation in characterization and then is a time when she wants to forget her past and question its beings, as we find in *Jasmine*; talking to Darrel, in search of a particular word for an Indian equivalent: "You mean Hindi, not Indian,. there is no such thing as Indian"(10). Such writing use their Diasporic status as a ploy to keep their identity separate, they dislike to recognize in India distinct cultures represented by several Indian languages—a multicultural phenomenon. Diaspora writing directly reflects the immigrant experience that comes out of immigrant settlement. Uma Parameswaran has defined it very cautiously:

> . . . the first is one of nostalgia for the homeland left behind mingled with fear in strange land. The second is a phase in which one is so busy adjusting to the new environment that there is little creative output. The third phase is the shaping of Diaspora existence by involving themselves in ethno cultural issues. The fourth is when they have 'arrived' and start participating in the larger world of politics and national issues. (ALB, Vol, I, No, 2, p.165)

That is why her work bears involvement with reality, a sense of wonder and fear, acute nostalgia as in *The Door I Shut behind Me* and *Trishanku and Other Writings*. The pull of past is so strong that throughout her works it appears and reappears and she laments, "When we leave our country we shut many doors behind ourselves though we are not aware of it at the time," and yet "there are many doors ahead of us," (Parmeswaran, 1998, 105). She cannot abandon her past and her Diasporic consciousness carries its history) philosophy and vision; she cannot come over Sita, Meera, Savitri, Rama, Lakshman and Jatayu, stick to Indian legend and myth and collaborates Indian culture; she cannot compromise with the present, as Shared says in *Sons Must Die and Other Plays*:

> It upsets me profoundly to find myself in a crowd. All those alien faces staring at or through you. It makes me wonder, makes me ask myself, what am I doing here?—Each so self contained, complete, looking at me as though I should not be there. (Parmeshwaran, 1998, 82)

And the next moment, the son retorts, ". . . our people, our old country, Dad, there's no 'our people' and no 'old country' for anyone in the world any more, least of all for us. This is our and here we shall stay"(Parmeshwaran, 1998, 83). Here lies the clash between the past and the present, the two generations, concern for root and rootlessness, native land and new land, preoccupation and the third space, singular culture and multicultural (cultural synthesis)—and such trend continues in all Diasporic writing.

Meena Alexander is another name who may be mentioned in this regard. Like other Diasporic writers she is aware of displacement, homelessness, fragmentation of identity, dislocation, origin, race, culture and nationality too. Her prose works *Manhattan Music, Nampally Road.* And *The Shock of Arrival: Reflections on Postcolonial Experience* vindicate her stand whereas *Fault lines: A Memoir* unfolds her inner self. *Manhattan Music* introduces with characters like Sandhya, Draupadi, Rashid and Jay, situated in different stages of exiles; Sandhya is in voluntary exile who compiles to the societal dictates of accompanying her husband to her homeland; Draupadi inherits the complex from her parents; Rashid battles constantly with his memories of home; and Jaya permanent nomad for whom home or motherland is a meaningless entity. Though in exile Sandhya never recovers from the ongoing of her motherland; the repercussions of Indian politics influences her sketches, her own image placed in her hometown. The racial taunting is disturbing to him and she gathers the sense of insecurity; horrifying memories disturb him; and her life becomes terrible nightmares reluctantly resigning to fate. To Sandhya, New York does not provide soothing experience. in her loveliness she is "afloat in the city" (3), her "memory swelling like black water threatened to drawn her" (4). She has to face hyphenated identities, divided loyalties and fragmented dreams, rushes to her Egyptian lover for solace and strive hard to save her father. To Draupadi, these things matter least she is of a different make, "born in America epitome of newness" (3). She is aware of her family history, class disorientation, colour discriminations, multiple dislocations and homelssness, *Manhattan Music* raises all these problems, fails to solve them and finally compromises providing no solutions at all. *Nompally Road* has a young woman as its protagonist, Mira whose homeland does not help her to translate her Romantic philosophy to become a writer and falsify the concept of nationalism, where Gandhi becomes meaningless and the rape of a poor Muslium woman Rameiza by a group of policemen is the stark reality. Now the question is that of ideology, of socialism, of commitment, of nationalism, of culture and of utopian framework of colonial discomfort and postcolonial achievements. *Fault Lines* is an autobiographical sketch that centres on the question of identity, home, culture and the postcolonial constructions; she pronounces, "I always felt that what I really was being left out as an Indian woman, I felt that I had to go back to India" (25). "I carry that world around with me. . . writing poems that are rooted in this soil and this landscape, in a village in South India. It is as if by doing this I can reconstitute whit is critical for me and nourish myself" (23). "My grandfather was a great idealist who really believed that there was a new India waiting, a new world based on issues like land reform and equality for all people. I had this extraordinary world available to me" (23-24) and later on she finds "my voice imprecise, my ignorance that of a perpetual immigrant, a woman with nowhere to lay her head" (32). *Shock of Arrival* is yet another autobiographical narrative which furnishes gateways into Meena's psyche presented in fictional characters the grief of homelessness. Meena puts together cultures languages as well as genres to highlight her experience of Diasporic self.

Jhumpa Lahiri is yet another name, though from a distant land, voices Diasporic sensibility very truly. Her *Interpreter of Maladies* has bagged several prizes, at the same time, it has also invited bitter criticism from a few corners too, such as poverty-stricken material', 'absence of depth', 'no amount of craft and skill in language or descriptive details'; 'void at the be art of original conception'; a misfit for 'greatening of life'; 'lacking in high seriousness' no graph of life' excess of value of farm over value of content: etc. It is a collection of nine stories, of 'mini India' settled abroad, battling with the same complex as we find in other Diasporic writings: nuances of cultural interactions, native consciousness, imposed life style, human despair, psychic dilemma, marital discord, loneliness, seclusion unsolved crisis, emotional frigidity, etc.

Marital discord of New England forms the gist of *A Temporary Matter* which rests for a while with the birth of a new child and ends with his death; modernity takes away the luster of value based life and the mother remains a relic of the past. Maladjustment continues in *The Interpreter of Maladies* accompanied by infidelity. "When Mr. Rizada came to Dine" is a passive political report, valuable for its characterization. *A*

Real Darwan exposes the vanity and escapist tendency ingrained in human nature, ridicules the residents of the flat who kick out Boori Ma (the symbol of maternal love and care, though incapacitated by senility), looking for a real durwan; Lahiri's derision and approbation go together. The story "Sexy" is display of sexual behavior of women at different levels, perhaps the desire and passion of human being with unlimited frontiers based on Freudian explanation. "Ms. Seris" tells us about the snobbery of the New Englanders, loneliness of Indian woman and the uncomfortable transplantation of alien culture. *The Blessed House* is a centre of compromises, sacrifices and adjustments, necessary for a sweet home. We find social satire in *The Treatment of Bibi Haldar*, human life defined in a new way. Human relationship and its different modes have been explained in *Third and Final Continent*. Precisely these stories are an attempt to negotiate the two cultures with varying degrees of success, their attitudes, their concerns, and their life styles; centring on social preoccupations such as love, marriage, marital discord, extramarital affairs, old age, illness, poverty and death. Like most of the Diasporic fiction, Jhumpa engages herself in exposing the conflict of culture, maladjustment) loneliness uncomfortable relationships, sexual adventures and urgency of, home with final resolution, "Now, I am free to discover life as I please.", as Bibi says in *The Treatment of Bibi Haldar*. As usual dilemmas remain unsolved, conflicts unsettled, complexities unread and questions unanswered.

Rohinton Mistry also follows the same pattern and his *Tales from Firozsha Baag* presents the smiles and tears, bickering and blessings of I whole line of Parsi Indians in Canada. Instances of 'otherness' steeped in India is present in "Ghost of Firozsha Baag"; "Squatter" deals with maladjustment leading to misadventure; "Lend Me Your Light" talks of displacement, contradictions and ambiguities—and all of them constitute a multicultural saga of defeat importance. The protagonist of "Swimming Lessons" and "Squatter" shuttles between Bombay and Toronto and the nation of 'otherness' and 'outsiders' haunts them. In "Lend Me Your Light" Kersi never loses his identity as he belongs to the middle class whereas the upper class Jamshed adopts the American dream and develops distaste for India; Percy remains consistent. Kersi reveals his inner self, "My entire burden of ridden and puzzles, unsolved... . I Tiresias, throbbing between two lives, humbled by the ambiguities and dichotomies confronting me" (TFB, 192); Jamshed lives in 'confusion, disdain, arrogance'. All characters of the stories recollect the Diasporic anxiety in one way or the other. My proposition is to ratiocinate the repetitive trend of Indian Diasporic fiction.

Now the question in whether such Diasporic writers (we may call them post-colonial) intend to rewrite nationalism (in some other way) to empower indigenous traditions and cultures, depreciated by a colonial past, as a voice of the subalterns (the doubly displaced) or it is simply the outburst of challenges of displaced mass regarding identity formation class-conflict nationalism and cultural dissemblance. Yes, expatriate Indian write with a sense of shared culture and shared history. In fact, the Diaspora is a theoretical formulation that explains questions regarding cultural identity and literary representations. If we calculate truly, we find in these Diasporic writers accepted oneness of culture, sought to be pronounced, from A.K. Ramanujan to Meena Alexander, from Salman Rushdie to Bharati Mukherjee and from Gayatri Spivak to Homi Bbabba. This exile bas been defined variously. Edward Said calls it "one of the saddest fates" (*Reflections*, 47) dislocation or an 'in-betweenness' (*Representations*, 52-58), 'away from family and familiar places, but also meant being a sort of permanent outcast, some one who never felt at home, and was always at odds with environment, inconsolable about the past, bitter about the present and the future (Said, *Reflections*, 47). In this definition we have answers of the particular trend of Diasporas writings. About the autobiographical tool, Leigh Gilmor points out, "Autobiography demonstrates that we can never recover the past, only represent it"(86). "These writers have to face the dominant feeling of 'otherness' and 'outsider' in a "state of being fully adjusted" (Said, 53); they fail to "take up life and become I citizen of just anywhere" (Said, 62) yet Said is not of the view that being exiled "is to be totally cut off, isolated hopelessly, separated from your place of origin" (Reflections, 48); the immigrant live, "neither completely at one with the new setting nor fully disencumbered of the old, beset with half involvements and half detachments) nostalgic and sentimental on one level, an adept mimic or a secret outcast on another" (Said, *Reflections*, 49).

In "Imaginary Homelands" Salman Rushdie says "exiles or emigrants or expatriates are haunted by some sense of loss, some urge to reclaim, to look back. We will not be capable of reclaiming precisely the thing that was lost" (10); "he discovers himself and other expatriates not as gods but wounded creatures cracked lenses, capable only of fractured perceptions" (12). If we provide the Diasporic writings the safe shelter of post colonialism, once again. it may be read as "a free floating metaphor for cultural embattlement and as an almost obsolete signifier for the historicity of race"(Suleri, 247).

It is not surprising to explain in simple words, one of the most complex formations of space in human history is the emergence of the multicultural space and under this scenario, a writer has to accept it, as M.G. Vassanji tells J.C. Bill in an interview, "We lived through a period of transitions and big change moments across continents, from India to Africa and within Africa and go on plus the personal changes within your lives the political changes, colonialism, wars, independence revolution—and you had to find out why you were, what you were, what happened to you; it's like coming out of a state of shock, trying to remember what happened during the last hundred years. In this horrible new crisis a writer cannot afford to do or discard mark.

Works Cited

Abdullah, M. & Ray Matthew, *The Time of the Peacock*, August & Rob, 1973.

Bhabha, H.K., *The Location of Culture*, London, Routledge, 1994.

Bill, J. C., 'Taboos: M.G. Vassanji', *The Power to Bend Spoons: Interviews with Canadian Novelistls*, (ed.), Beverly Damio, Toronto Mereury Press, 1988.

Braziel, J. E., *Doaspora, an Introduction,* Blackwell Pub., USA, 2008.

______ and Anita Mannur, *Theorizing Diaspora: A Reader,* Oxford: Blackwell, 2002.

Clark & Mukherjee, *Days and Nights in Calcutta*, New York, Dobleday, 1977.

Cohen, Robin, *Global Diasporas: An Introduction*, Seattle: Univ. Of Washington Press, 1997.

Cyril, C., *The Ganga and its Tributaries*, Victoria: Mcphee Gribble, 1993.

Docker, J., *The Poetics of Diaspora,* Continuum, London & New York, 2001.

Huggan, G., *The Postcolonial Exotic: Marketing the Margins*, London, Routledge, 2001.

Hutcheon, L., *The Canadian Post-modern*, Toronto, OUP, 1988.

Jayram, N., *The Indian Diaspora*, Sage Pub., New Delhi, 2004.

Jung, C.G., *The Integration of the Personality*, translated by Standey Dell, Lowe and Brydone Printers Ltd., London, 1940.

Karnath, K.S., *My Concern for Life and Literature*, Sahitya Akademi, 1990.

Lahiri, J., *Interpreter of Maladies*, New York: Houghton Mifflin, 1999.

Leigh, G., *Autobiographies: A Feminist Theory of Self Representation,* Ithaca; C.U.P., I993.

Marcuse, H., *Eros and Civilization*, London, Rutledge, 1956.

Mcleod, A.L., *The Literature of Indian Diaspora,* Sterling Pub., New Delhi, 2000.

Mistry, R., *Tales from Firozsha. Baag*, Penguin, 1987.

Mukherjee, B., 'A Four Hundred Years old Woman', in Janet Steenburgen. *The Writer on Her Work II*, New York, Norton, 1992.

_______*Darkness*, Toronto, Penguin, 1985.

_______*Jasmine*, Harmondsworth, Penguin, 1990.

Naipaul. V.S., *Guerrillas*, Hammondsport, Penguin, 1977.

Nandan, S., *Requiem for a Rainbow*, Canberra, Pacific Indian Pub., 2001.

Parameswaran, U., *Trishanku and other Writings*, New Delhi, Prestige, 1998.

_______*Sons Must Die and Other Plays*, New Delhi, Prestige, 1998.

Paranjape, M., (Ed)., *I am Diaspora: Theories Histories, Texts*, New Delhi, Indian Pub., 2001.

Rushdie, S., *Imaginary Homelands, Essays and Criticism:* 1981-1991, London; Granta, 1992.

Safran, William, Diaspora in Modern Socities : Myth of Homeland and Return, *Diaspora*, 1991.

Said, E.W., *Orientalism*, London, Penguin, 1978.

_______'Intellectual Exile: Expatriates and Marginals', *Representation of the Intellectual: The 1993 Reith Lectures*, New York; Pantheon, 1994.

_______'Reflections on Exile', *Out There: Marginalization and Contemporary Cultures,* (ed.), R. Ferguson, et al., Cambridge Mass; MIT Press, 1990.

Satchidanandan, K., *Authors, Texts, Issues,* 2003, Pencraft International, NewDelhi.

Suleri, S., Woman Skin Deep: Feminism and the Postcolonial Condition, *Critical Inquiry* 18.2 (1992).

Thieme, J., 'V.S. Naipaul's Third World, '*The Journal of Commonwealth Litrature,* August, 1975.

2

Considerations of Diaspora Writing

The flourishing pattern of Diasporic writing, which is substantial, significant and complex writing, makes it necessary to revise the cultural theories of nation, race, and identity that has been termed, in recent times, as Diasporic Studies and Transnational Studies. It covers the writers of Indian origin settled in countries such as the US, Canada, England, Australia, Caribbean, Africa, Far East and other parts of the world. Such writings attract regular ongoing critical consideration. These writers have come to terms with the Diasporic spaces they inhabit and relate to the Indian inheritance and their writings put the core issues of Diasporic discourse in bold relief.

Amit Chaudhery is of the opinion that the true moment for the expatriate writing as well as Indian English Writing can be traced back to 1981, the year which saw Rushdie's novel *Midnight's Children's* publication and winning of the Booker Prize. Strictly speaking, the Diaspora Indian English Writers cannot be bracketed as a monolithic category forming a homogeneous alliance rather it is a composite cultural context, banking on the stuff gathered from different nations, cultures, societies but Indian sensibility as a common string. It has been also observed that their empathy and credentials with India is also of shifting degrees of intensity ranging from ranging from the recollections of the past and the compulsions of the present; we may term this as 'infinite shades of Diasporic difference'. Prof. T. Vinoda is of the view:

> In general, the situation of these writers enables them to leverage their experience of living on the cusp of cultures, their happy / unhappy positioning bestowing upon them a privileged perspective of outsider/insider, mixing cultural memory with desire in a hundred different ways. Most of the time, their marginality in host nations enables them to strike a chord of homelessness of the modern individual. Their writings range from expression of postcolonial angst, immigrant experience, caught–on-the-cusp syndrome or outsider/insider perspectives—what probably accounts for the international acclaim is their cosmopolitan hybridity combined with a refreshingly new, bold and creative idiom. (Vinoda & Shailja, 2006, 13)

And now we have an array of international awards, such as, the Nobel Prize, the Booker Prize, the Booker of the Booker, the Pultizer, the Commonwealth Prize, the National Book Award, the Orange Prize, The Giller Prize, The Betty Trask Prize, etc. Besides, the old 'melting pot' ideology has been substituted by the theory of multiculturalism in the modern societies accommodating the Diaspora as the 'other'. This is the age of the 'transplanted world' in which 'heterogeneity and mongrelisation' have been accepted as "an article of cultural faith, a core value and the central principle of life" furnishing the epistemological backdrop and raising intricate questions of belonging, identity and citizenship governing the mindset of globalisation and mapping out its terrain. These writings redefine home, homelessness, belonging, loss and identity with possible reservations and prejudices. It also questions the hegemonic structures of the post-colonial era with a sustained effort of rewriting history, the Diasporic obsessions, the Eurocentric construction of thought, the multi-layered 'heteroglossic referetiality' of the language, the mutating configurations of the lived experiences, the objective correlative for his allegories of personal histories, subjectivity of the writers in interpretations of personal lives and public events to examine the present, challenges of the canon, projection of the contemporary history through myths, allegories, burlesque and parody, explorations of alternative histories, etc.

Most of these writings are nostalgic recollections; an atavistic reversion of old practices left behind in the homeland especially since liberal multiethnic settings they live in make space for the 'other'. It also leads to custom-package ethnic practices for the curious western readers, termed as 'memory-feed to judicious writerly uses'. In some writings we find inalienable affiliation with the distinct regional Indian culture, as that of Bengal in the case of Jhumpa Lahiri, Amit Chaudhuri, Amitav Ghose, Bharati Mukherjee, Chitra Divakaruni and Sunetra Gupta—they reconstruct the old places and practices with the help of memory and desire which is poignant and intense, though they do not induce India through standard cultural signifier, similar to the writers of the regional language. It may have another purpose as that of the celebration of their origin or 'multilocationality across geographical, cultural and psychical boundaries'. Such women writers may have the impact of the cultural schism, caused by dislocation, defining her as 'a new being in the Diasporic setting', away from the indigenous traditions, folklore, cultural values and social practices. Above all the expatriate sensibility is common to all the settings with a possible incursion of the Western philosophies like existentialism and the intersection of the Orient and the West. Such intersections, of Diasporic dislocations and disjunctures are exclusive to the Diasporic writings only and not possible with the vernacular native writers. To some critics such representations of Indian reality tend to be inauthentic, myopic and faithless as it does not cover the locational terrain. With a sense of loss and homelessness comes the fortitude and indomitable spirit of 'dislocation, disjunction, instability and double vision' as the distinguishing characteristic of the Diasporic writing—an attempt to redefine the self and redraw the boundary. Jasbir Jain traces its origin on the literary scene from the beginning of writing, "right from the *Mahabharata,* the *Ramayana* and the Biblical travels through the Bhakati pilgrimages and wars of conquest."

Precisely, the term expatriate sensibility is a legitimate literary term that refers to a complex state of mind and emotion, including the yearning for the past, pang of homelessness, the feeling of alienation and rootlessness, the compulsions of cultural dilemmas, the experience of hostility in the alien land, the rejection of his ethnic identity, the consequence depression, frustration and cultural shock and the cultural conflict. To elucidate our argument we can go for a few writers such as Salman Rushdie, Amitav Ghosh and V.S. Naipaul.

Salman Rushdie appeared on the global literary horizon with a big bang and his first novel *Midnight's Children* (1981) proved to be an outstanding novel of the period, According to Prof. M. K. Naik, this novel was:

> A multifaceted narrative, it is at once an autobiographical *bildungsroman*, a picaresque comedy, a surrealist fantasy, a political and existential allegory, a topical satire and a stylistic experiment—an exciting blend of the natural and the supernatural, political allegory and ethical implications." (Naik & Narayan, 2009, 2004-4)

Rushdie himself calls it 'a sort of modern fairy tale' (204). His other major works include *Haroun and the Sea of Stories*'(1990), *The Satanic Verses* (1988), *Shame* (1983), *The Moor's Last Sigh*(1995), *The Ground Beneath Her Feet* (1999), etc. William Walsh feels that the "huge purpose of *Midnight's Children* is the personification and realisation of Indian life" (Walsh, 1983, 257).

Rosalind opines:

> *Midnight's Children* is a book about India that must be felt, seen, and reacted in all its varied texture, overlapping mythologies, fabulous fantasies and harsh realities—a piece of 'fiction-faction' by one born in India but settled abroad and tries to reconceptualise the dichotomy between personal and national identity in a way that made a new kind of social engagement possible. (112)

It is a story of about 63 years of India's pre- and post-colonial twentieth century history exposing the prominent events of partition, etc. The three generations of Sinai family have the varied experience of being at Srinagar, Amritsar, Agra, and Bombay, shifting to Karanchi. Saleem Sinai is the narrator of the story writing in the night and working in the daytime at a pickle factory. This narrative has a cynical progression going to the past in retrospective manner and operating in Saleem' memory only. It presents a cross-section of humanity of Indians-Muslins-Anglo Indians as tripartite. It begins in the midnight of August 14-15, 1947, running to Jallianwallah Bagh, Saleem's birth, Indo-Pak War and Emergency in March 1977. In this novel Rushdie is 'no dispassionate, disinterested chronicler' like the protagonist Saleem and trims the history as per the demand of the novel; in *Imaginary Homelands* he defends, "in fiction what actually happened is less important than what the author can manage to persuade his audience believe" (271). In *Express Magazine,* 20 March, 1983, in her essay *A Legend out of Subcontinent* Meenakshi Mukherjee says, "the notion has first to be imagined to become real—*Midnight's Children* presents memory's truth—has its own reality, its heterogeneous but usually coherent version of events; and no same human being ever trusts someone else's version more than his own."

A. Rosalind uses a metaphorical language when he says that "in surprisingly numerous ways India is Saleem Sinai and Saleem Sinai is India" (116). And it is here that the nostalgic flavour of Rushdie's talent is evident, for instance, "the clock ridden, crime stained birth"(4), Sinai's "map face"(144), "sky blue eyes",(145) "something lacking in the chin"(144) Saleem's "sinuses also puffed up" (359), "a state of acute crisis"(360), "her tartness's smile"(370). Rushdie is a critical historian and hence he teases the spirit of India in altogether different way. Saleem's past admits the significance of the traditions of democratic and representative forms of government, "the teeming millions of the Indian forgotten, populace, the creative power of the imagination to construct our reality and narratives, and finally his utterance, to understand just one life, you have to swallow the whole world"(126). Rushdie uses the theme of the duality of all reality condensed in Saleem-Shiva motif, the two form the split halves of a single-self, joined together by a prophecy (87) —they embody the split in the educated Indian's orientation to life wrought by the western influence. Saleem's destiny bows to woman and history (133) indicating the essential connection between Mother India and mother figures he comes across and says:

> Women have made me; and also unmade. It is perhaps, a matter of connection: is not Mother India, Bharat Mata, commonly thought of as female? And as you know there is no escape from her (483)

Saleem's self-consciousness which understands his 'too-many women' as the dynamic aspect of *Maya*, as cosmic energy, which is represented as the female organ, seeking to relate to "the multiple faces of Bharat Mata" (485). Saleem's use of the image of mother is typical of Indian mind set-up; his treatment of Mary, Mumtaz, Vinita, Padma and finally the image of Kali felt in the destructive mother destroying his fertility and performing the dance of death. Rushdie's complex relationship with India is visible in his presentation of India as mother, mother as ambiguity, India as woman of orthodoxy and superstition and the writer's disclosure of the fact that Indian society has respect for money, position and power (83).

Rushdie symbolises the post-Independence India with Methwold's estate: while the bureaucracy inherits one kind of power there is a transfer of power on Methwold's estate and the Western influence is seen in Ahmed Sinai's adoption of false Oxford drawl and bottles of gin, Lila Sabarmati's pianola, the boy Saleem's 'stethoscoped English Milord'. The urban India gets reflected in the speech patterns of dialogue with typical Indian stresses, intonations and syntax, for instance the expletives like 'Allah', 'whats its name', 'arre baba', 'writery-shitery'; the sentences are also Indian like, for instance, "Arre baba eatna, ok, starve starve, who cares two pice"; there are puns on Indian names like Maharani of Cooch Nahin, Dr.Sharabi, Lifafa Das, etc.

Rushdie maintains that the English language ceased to be the sole possession of the English some time ago ('The Empire Writes Back with a Vengeance', *London Times,* 3 July 1982). The development of India is visible in the growth of Saleem', amidst a barren and hostile world, his burden of history, his representation of the intellectual, his imaginative Indian being able to think, feel and communicate, with a mind of, a sort of, parliament of various viewpoints, idealistic, deeply interested in the surrounding population of men and women, his moral stance, his hatred for fanaticism and communalism and his fertile imagination with sincerity, love and tolerance.

The world of this novel is ironic, quirky and grave, and Saleem preserves his identity of being Indian. The state of Emergency is presented with traumatic experiences and then the lifting of emergency is also presented. The most important survivor is Aadam Sinai born during Emergency as Saleem was born into Independence and he represents the second generation as a synthesis of Shiva and Saleem, a more pragmatic spinner of a new myth after the failure of the myth of freedom, religion and money; both Saleem and Aadam are a assortment of the history of the history the Indian Colonials as well as contemporary India. Aadam is aware of his hybridity and so destiny and nation does not matter to him as Saleem is; it is a heart-rending quest of identity.

In *Imaginary Homelands* Rushdie admits, "The story of Saleem does indeed lead him to despair. But the story is told in a manner designed to echo, as closely as my abilities allowed, the Indian talent for non-stop self regeneration." (16) He further elaborates, "This is why, the narrative constantly, throws up new stories, why it 'teems'. The form multitudinous hinting at the infinite possibilities of the country– is the optimistic counter weight to Saleem's personal tragedy. I do not think that a book written in such a manner can really be called a departing work."(16) Here we find the allegorical parallel of the growth to maturity of the individual and the growth of an independent India which has been the recurrent theme of most of the works of Rushdie.

Rushdie's nostalgic flight stimulated him to create the Indian Subcontinent trilogy of *Midnight's Children, Shame* and *The Moor's Last Sigh*, the first two revolves round politics in India with a grain of politics of Pakistan whereas *Shame* is entirely about Pakistan, its social and political interwoven. O.P. Mathur is of the view that:

> Rushdie attempts to make it more powerfully incisive by veiling it beneath a number of artistic devices like exaggeration, symbolic portrayal, pretention and denial. Like the legendary Porteus, he frequently shifts his role

> as a narrator from a mere occasional objective chronicler to Thackeray's puppet-master, Dickens's displayer of human eccentricities, Anderson's teller of fairy tales, Fielding's delightful interpolator, Swift's allegorist, Poe's creator of mystery and the Elizabethan tragedian's reveller in bloodshed and revenge. Moreover, he is not always to be taken at his word for sometimes while, like a fundamentalist condemning the 'stone-washing' Indians who engineered the partition of Pakistan, he is playfully adopting this point of view. ... both the spatial and the chronological backgrounds of the novel are in harmony with the strangeness, abnormality, weirdness, bloodshed and suggestions of the supernatural that characterize the events and the persons inhabiting this world set at an angle from reality. The shamelessness of this world creates among the sensitive a feeling of shame or '*sharam*'. (200 - 01)

It is also established that *Shame* puts forth an 'avenging angel' to burn, and to destroy all moral and political evil in Rushdie's Pakistan, as contrasted to India which he regards as his spiritual homeland, for he was very angry when he learnt that his family's Bombay house had been sold, and for a property 'Anis Villa', he successfully fought a long-drawn out legal battle. Rushdie carries with him tolerant, democratic and humanitarian values of Indian society that is why, he calls *Shame* "a document about myself in India", and makes it more clear in *Midnight's Children:*

> ... the difference between my Indian childhood and Pakistani adolescence is that in the first I was beset by an infinity of the alternative realities, while in the second, I was adrift, disoriented, amid an equally infinite number of falseness, unrealities and lies. (389)

In this novel, he brings out the reality of Pakistan through a dual strategy of mockery and horror. We find the same kind of strong feeling in the concluding lines of Taslima Nasrin's *Lajja*:

> ... it was almost dawn and through the cracks in the window, sunlight streamed in. Sudhamoy said, 'Come, let us go away.' Suranjena could not conceal his surprise.
>
> 'Where will we go Baba? he asked.

> Sudhamoy said, 'India'.
>
> And his voice cracked as the shame swept over him. But he had said it, he had forced it out, he had compelled himself to say that they would go and he had realized that was the way it would have to be because the strong mountain that he had built within himself was crumbling day by day. (216)

Both Rushdie and Taslima have strong Indian ideological roots and prefer Indian values, though they are forced to live abroad and their ulterior wish is to allow the sunlight of love to flood their respective countries, the whole subcontinent or even the world as pronounced by Taslima in the *Epigraph* to *Lajja,* "Let Another Name For Religion be Humanism."

In this connection Rushdie's collection of short stories, *East West* (1994) is more significant, because it echoes, ironically of course, the proverbial rhetoric of Empire *East, West, Home's Best* (Grant,1999, 100)—it is a discourse built on the myths of Empire and the notion of England forever as 'home' wherever in the world you may be. The narrator of the short story *The Courter* explains:

> But I, too, have ropes around my neck; I have them to this day, pulling me this way and that. East and West, the nooses tightening, commanding, choose, choose. I buck, I snort, I whinny, I kick—I choose neither of you, and both. Do you hear? I refuse to choose.(211)

In the post-colonial late twentieth century Diasporic reading it has been a common stance to talk of 'home' as increasingly mobile, enacting a deterritorialization that can be both a blessing and a curse, at the same time, it is both illusionary and fictional place constructed through the myths and fragments of the migrant imagination. The concept of 'home' and 'abroad' is that of shifting and ambivalent boundaries and occupies the soul of Rushdie's work (as creation of *Utopian* fantasy) as evident in *Grimus* (1975), the trilogy of *Midnight's Children, Shame* and *The Moor's Last Sigh,* and *The Satanic Verses* (1988). In all these works we find his imaginary homelands caught between the East and West explorations of the anxiety and transformation of migrant experience, and the myth of migration and transformation. Following the publication of voluntary *The Satanic Verses* (1988) and after the *fatwa* the voluntary self-exile or banishment of Rushdie, it was the time of political and social upheavals and contradictions, though he found himself away from 'my community' (that of homeland) and 'from India, from everyday life', in a cultural suspension, caught in a limbo split between East and West, that of cultural implicit, a mongrelisation fed by an emotional and intellectual identification with the culture of the past. I. Hamilton in his book *The First Life of Salman Rushdie* discloses the secret of his life when he says, "It's true that even now I feel 'at home' in Bombay, in particular, in a way I don't feel anywhere else in the world today"(111). Rushdie keeps on oscillating between 'here' and 'there', between East and West and fails to define 'home' as such. This dilemma dramatizes the cultural complexities of transplantation, inherent in the losses and gains of 'immigrant translations' and also move the question of culture's appropriation beyond the assimilationist's dream, or, the racist's nightmare. Critics are of the view that these Diasporic writers have undergone cultural metamorphosis by inventing alternative strategies of survival and by reconfiguring the monolithic notion of the imperial motherland. Stuart Hall is of the view that:

> Such new and post-war Diasporas often inhabit two identities—speak two cultural languages ... translate and negotiate between them—without simply by assimilating to them and losing their identities completely—the traces of the particular cultures, traditions and languages and histories by which they were shaped. (310)

Toni Morrison's well known dictum of blacking or universalizing out may be quoted here, enabling the 'out there' to exist alongside the 'in here' against 'binary logic of exclusivism', living in 'heterogeneous category'. Rushdie has become a metaphor both in his fiction and in his critical essays where the trope of migrancy has become renowned for representing a particular way of seeing which Bharati Mukherjee terms in 'Introduction' to *Darkness* as "partially comprehending the world"(3). In *Shame* Rushdie says, "My has created a narrator who claims to represent Pakistan by slices in fragments of broken mirrors," as he adds:

> The country in this story is not Pakistan, or not quite. There are two countries, real and fictional, occupying the same space. My story, my fictional country exists, like myself at a slight angle to reality. I have found this off-centring to be necessary, but its value is, of course, open to debate. My view is that I am not writing only about Pakistan. (29)

Obviously, the narrator questions the legitimacy of the authority of his own view as 'Outsider! Trespasser!', he also says:

> I tell myself this will be a novel of leave-taking, my last word on the East from which, many years ago, I began to come loose. I do not believe myself when I say this. It is a part of the world to which whether I like it or not I am still joined. (28)

As a post-colonial writer Rushdie universalized the state of homelessness as central to the concept of post modernity. He reiterates the 'stereoscopic vision' of the Diaspora and their status of being 'out-of-country' and 'out-of-language' and says:

> The Indian writer, looking back to India, does so through guilt-tinted spectacles. (I am, of course, once more, talking about myself.) I—am now speaking of those of us who emigrated—and I suspect that there are times when the move seems wrong to us all, when we seem to ourselves post lapsarian men and women. We are Hindus who have crossed the black water; we are Muslims who eat pork—we are now partly of the west. Our identity is at once plural and partial. Sometimes we feel that we straddle two cultures; at other times, we fall between two stools—but however ambiguous and shifting this ground may be, it is not an infinite territory for a writer to occupy. (79)

Another Diaspora writer under discussion is Amitav Ghosh who has been the winner of Sahhitya Akademi Award in 1989 and the prestigious Prix Midicis Etrangere award, whereas he is also known for declining the Commonwealth Literature Prize (for *The Glass Palace*, 2000). His famous works include *The Shadow Lines, The Circle of Reason, In an Antique Land, The Calcutta Chromosome, The Count Down and The Glass Palace. The Circle of Reason* (1986) is "punctuated by miracles and eccentricities, but it fails to generate adequate thematic substance" (Naik & Narayan, 2009, 204). *In An Antique Land* (1992) "demonstrates how history can be enriched by imaginative reconstruction of the past" (Naik & Narayan, 2009, 209). *The Glass Palace* (2000), "deals with the final days of Thebaw, the last king of Burma" (Naik & Narayan, 2009, 209) and *The Shadow Lines* (1988) has at least a recognisable narrative framework. His *The Calcutta Chromosomes* (1996) won the Arthur C. Clarke Award for science fiction, though it has a mystery, a ghost story and a dystopia.

For our present study we can go for his novel *The Hungry Tide* which has a confusing ending:

> You know—for me, home is where the Orcella are: so, there's no reason why this couldn't be it.
>
> And the reply was—
>
> That's the difference between us. For me home is where I can brew a pot of good tea. (400)

Here the 'home' is being defined with two different ideologies and worldviews. Life is the totality of social, familial, religious and historical experience, taken together and it is reflected in *The Hungry Tide*. Ghosh has to come back to his birth place in search of his location of setting and articulate his calculations. The novel opens with the Ganges, a prominent Indian myth, a geographically familiar terrain and then follows Sunderbans, Bay of Bengal, the Himalayas, etc. Moreover, these are the terrible junctures to profess that nature and man are locked in conflict, the mischievous rivers playing havoc in the mainland and out to merge into the Bay of Bengal like different traditions with 'cataclysmic chaotic orders,' the vibrant exposure of the tidal ecology. Symbolically it is the integration of the human and natural worlds, the conceptual and social worlds, and the modern and primitive worlds that bring about natural catastrophes. Ghosh does not go for anything new; rather he is indulged in the reconstruction of the past only which include regional and local references, legends of the place, the primitivistic symbology, religious personifications, etc. It is here that we may recall Edward Said's *Reflections on Exile*, where he says:

> "Exile is strangely compelling to think about but terrible to experience. It is the unbearable rift forced between a human being and a native place, between the self and its true home: its essential sadness can never be surmounted. (173)

In this novel, Kusum wants to reclaim her home and identity. For government a tiger is more important than man. The confluence of the Western trends and old values is focussed at every juncture. Ghosh identifies difference within culture and for his favourite blend is that of cultural change and cross fertilization od cultures. Actually, this novel has a story of world in transition, though this integrated world does not denote hegemony. Ghosh's journey towards home with the help of history, memory and past is the outcome of his inclination towards his home. Ernest Renan defines nation as:

> Two things, which in truth are but one, constitute this soul or spiritual principle (called nation). One lies in the past, one in the present. One in the possession in common of a rich legacy of memories; the other is present day consent, the desire to live together, the will to perpetuate the value of the heritage that one has received in undivided form. (Reman, 1990, 19-20)

Diasporic experience depends on the way it has been imbibed. D. Ratanagiri Usha opines:

> Articulating the expatriate experience is a sort of explaining 'the other'—'the other' being the psyche of the immigrant whose acceptance or negation of homeland, search for routes and identity, nostalgia and memory, hyphenated entity, sense of dislocation and loss and so on find expression in the fiction of the Diaspora Community over the past two decades. India with its remarkable cultural diversity and its people asserting their ethnic, religious, linguistic and racial identities continues to fascinate the diaspora writer. The antique land of tales, stories, myths, legends and puranas pulls the Indian immigrant writers to draw from its treasure house incessantly (Usha, 2006, 91).

Amitav Ghosh has been both an 'insider' and an 'outsider' as he frequents India and makes it a centrestage in all his works,

Calcutta being the prominent one. Ghosh is fond of 'human history and its predicament' because he is an anthropologist and historical researcher, and the human history is determined by religion, tradition and politics and thus he reconstructs and fabricates the thread of civilization across the land, be it that of Indian, Egyptian, Muslim, Jewish, etc. In the novel *In An Antique Land* the symbolic presentation of the minor incidents and trivial practices influence a large segment of religious tradition and social practices—that of violation of taboos, and sin, bringing communal violence and despise.

In this age of post-modern era, we talk of multiculturalism and plurality which ultimately lead to multiple truths and realities and history as a faithful record of events is challenged particularly of its objectivity, influencing the historical interpretation, making it ambiguous, incoherent and multilayered meaning. Salman Rushdie is of the view:

> Reality is built on our prejudices, misconceptions and ignorance as well as our perceptiveness and knowledge. The reading of Saleem's unreliable narration might be, I believed, a useful analogy for the way in which we everyday attempt to 'read' the world. (Rusdie, 1992, 25)

Rushdie has his own perception and so everyone of us has of looking at different things of the world and the world as a whole—and all these go in the making of our beliefs, thoughts, views, ideas, ideology, prejudices, etc.

Diaspora writing reviews history for its lost identities and missing links and dwells heavily on the 'Presence of the Past', in order to create a space for the marginalized and fractured decentred self, which is why Ghosh admits, "History is profound in my thought and in my novels", and this is possible for him by probing anthropology, geography, sociology, psychology and a bit of science. The best instance of such synthesis is *The Shadow Lines* where history is employed as a tool to interpret and understand the present. Tridib furnishes his felt essence to the unnamed narrator and it is true to great extent when he says:

> "One could never know anything except through desire, real desire, which was not the same thing as greed or lust;

> a pure, painful and primitive desire, a longing for everything that was not in oneself, a torment of the flesh, that carried one beyond the limits of one's mind to other times and other places and even if one was lucky to a place where there was no border between oneself and one's image in the mirror. (Ghosh, 1998, 29)

Historical and political events coincide with the happenings of personal lives in a paradoxical way and interpreted and reinterpreted by different characters in multiple perspectives to perception valuable and viable. The communal riot is explained in three different perspectives by three narrators; the riot in India and Dhaka are similar; for the narrator it is a struggle for survival, for Robi it persists as a sense of guilt, a nightmarish dream, he being a helpless spectator shattering sense of integrity and defining freedom as mirage in the riot-torn world; and for may a sense of grief out of her helplessness, bringing final redemption to the narrator and to herself. The same technique of recollecting past through memories is applied here; past is correlated to the present in search of alternative truth. Such details torment and liberate, confuse and interpret, shatter and gather simultaneously through zigzag movement in time and place, moving towards the future with the past and present as concurrent.

What is most striking is the sense of 'house' or 'home' in the novel as perceived in the imagination of the narrator, Tridib or Ila. For Tridib it should have place 'to fly kites', 'to hide when one wanted to sulk', 'to shout to one's friends', for the narrator the necessity of verandas was no more accountable than the need for doors and walls, and for Ila it meant a lot of freedom, gratifying her pride. It is Ghosh's version of reality and truth, self and the world, peeping through the window of the past.

The Hungry Tide projects the complexities of historical as well as contemporary relations between different classes of people exercising their communication skill as the most powerful English, the language of power, Bangla the local language, etc. Language stands in the role of locations, dislocation and relocation, significant in the global context. India is presented in its post-colonial context how the native masters crush the poor displaced. In the novel the memory of de-territorialisation of Morichjhapi in the past animates the desire for re-territorialisation in future in the Tidal lands by the concerted efforts of Nilima, Piya and the local community, led by a catastrophic struggle for a new lease of life, bulldozed by the politics of power belying the myth, religion, language and other belief systems claiming unification in society and the need for a symbiosis between human beings and Precisely, Ghosh is preoccupied with issues of hybridity, in-betweenness, morbidity and crossovers of ideas and identities; his characters are lost in the oblivion of the past, for instance, an obscure slave in *In an Antique Land*, a mysterious urchin in *The Calcutta Chromosome* and an overlooked fisherman in *The Hungry Tide*, all carved out of different situations at different junctures of time and space, oscillating between nostalgia and relief, terror and hope, violence and peace, and dream and reality.

The case of V. S. Naipaul is unique who could never identify himself either with India or Trinidad, India the land of origin and Trinidad, the land of his ancestors' exile—yet we bracket him under the bracket of Diaspora writers' community. As M.K. Naik writes:

> V.S. Naipaul's Indian ancestry is indisputable, but he is so much of an outsider when he writes about India and the Indians and so much of an insider while dealing with Carribean life and character, that there can be no two opinions on his rightful inclusion in the history of West Indian Writing. (Naik, 1999, 3-4)

Naipaul in an interview to *India Today* says, "India is an ancestral fascination, you cannot forget it," He is, primarily, a traveller but his travelogues speak volumes. When he begins his journey of self, he finds India to be 'an area of darkness', a nation with a 'wounded civilization' and a country which is disillusioned due to 'million mutinities'. His two years of stay in India and frequent visits opens before him the image of the country that is thoroughly corrupt and gravely effected by Westernisation. The country is forgetful of its glorious cultural legacy and has remained only 'a dot'. Subsequently, his wide travels across the world make him realize that the whole world is dark. India, the most fascinating land which had been the background of his childhood is unacceptable and unpreferable.

Naipaul is, a sort of, 'International Citizen', though he has abandoned Trinidad and England happened to be an alien land for him. Yet there is no corner in the world that he may claim to belong to him. His predicament makes the whole world dark for him. He, as a Diaspora writer, enjoys a unique stature as a prophet, a soothsayer and a doomwatcher who tells unpalatable truths looking through the creeds, cultures and post-colonial societies; he strips them of their pretence and defence mechanisms by means of irony and prophecy. The Conardian vision is central to his writings as his feelings of "lost souls, lost countries and a vision of the world's half made societies as places which continuously made and unmade themselves, where there was no goal"(Naipaul, 1983, 208). His comment on postcolonial societies include his books on India. His cold and critical eyes analyses customs, tradition and cultures as a third generation immigrant caught up in a tension between the mythical and historical realties about the country. In *An Area of Darkness*, he says:

> Hysteria had been my reaction and a brutality dictated by a new awareness of myself as a whole human being and a determination, touched with fear, to remain what I was, it mattered little through whose eyes I was seeing the East; there had as yet been no time for this type of self-assessment. (13)

He moves through the 'area of darkness' and self-analysis and monitoring of responses ensue from him, and he came to know that racial similarities is meaningless and his Trinidadian upbringing and Western Education has rendered him a colonial without a country, as a product of an empire already withdrawn. He adopts a pragmatic approach in *India: A Wounded Civilization* to prove his point on the postcolonial society, its culture, concepts and assumptions, such as *Dharma* and *Karma* at the back of Hindu attitude. For him Gandhi and R.K. Narayan represent old morality and Vijay Tendulkar and U.S. Anantmurti the 'new morality', whereby individuals realizing the inadequacy of past myths strike out on their own. He says: India is for me a difficult country; it isn't my home and cannot reject it or be different to it" (Naipaul, 1979, 8). He finds himself in spiritual fix, not of divided loyalties but of divided energies. In *India: A Million Mutinies Now* he likens himself in far-off countries and came to India as a foreigner, without any prejudice:

> Growing up in far-off Trinidad, I had no idea of class or region, none of the supports and cushions of people in India. Like Gandhi, among the immigrant Indians of South Africa, and for much the same reasons, I have developed instead the idea of the family of India. And my attempt to come to terms with history, my criticism, my bewilderment and sorrow was tuned inward, focussing on the civilization and the social organization that had given so little protection. (Naipaul, 1998, 399)

Darshan Singh Maini diagnoses it as his 'complex fate' of being an Indian in a mixed colonial Trinidad, responsible for his final achievement and says:

> Without such a troubled heritage, he would be practically a disaffected and disengaged intellectual, converting his self hatred into an occupational play and living on it in transparent hauteur in the manner of our own inimitable Nirad C. Chaudhari. (Maini, 1984, 93-4)

His ambiguous entity results in a characteristic complexity of feeling in his attitude to human experience. He is aware of his Indian background for which he comes and is actually submerged in a mixed culture whose other components are equally eroded and twisted and it exercises an aggressive hold on people's sentiments. Both the West Indian and the East Indian cultures are products of cultural displacements, oppressed by a sense of dereliction. It is the absence of a well-defined tradition that promotes or necessitates such pragmatic qualities as cleverness, resourcefulness, common sense, and manipulations of people and circumstances. That is why all Naipaul's characters learn how to survive at all odds, in a colonial ethos, discovering one's potentialities. He is disinherited by all traditions, at the same time, exposed to all traditions and so his every move is an assertion of independence and identity.

In *The Middle Passage* he says, "Living in a borrowed culture, the West Indian, more than most, needs writers to tell him who is he and where he stands"(73). He further admits, "the act of writing is not merely a matter of self-expression but also an instrument of an awareness seeking to modify social reality" (Naipaul, 1972, 29). He departs from the constructive foreclosed background of the Carribbean Island to the open, literate and cosmopolitan with the portrayal of the predicament of the postcolonial individual. In an interview with Ian Hamilton, he says, "I've spent a lot of time—trying to define why one felt out of it, why one felt one didn't one didn't belong to this tradition of English letters. It was because its assumptions about the world were assumptions I could never make oneself."

Naipaul's writings is a continual revelation of his East Indian-West Indian identity of double exile and meditation on his Diasporic experience of post-imperial and post-colonial, as a psychic and symbolic sense of 'homelessness'. His writings has its moorings both in colonial and post-colonial trauma of the history as the psychic losses both as a participant and victim of the imperial process, located as twice born immigrant both within Trinidad and within Britain. The process of self-discovery starts here search of psychic and cultural equilibrium in the narratives of anxiety; that is why Naipaul calls his work as being caught in transitional space which he terms as "a kind of limbo (where) I am a refugee in the sense that I am always peripheral." His work dwels on 'obsolescence of his own discourse', displaying an 'anguish of affiliation' to the canonical house of Englishness which is both the source of his betrayal and the means of his potential liberation. The 'in-between' space has consistently bred ambivalence. Being caught 'in limbo' enables Naipaul a 'way of seeing', 'the excessive novelty of post colonial history' and 'the excessive anachronism of the canon'. No doubt, Naipaul is caught between the lure of the canonical 'house' of Englishness and the need to reconcile and comprehend the broader dimensions of his Diasporic inheritance. It is an illuminating paradigm for contemporary critics who attempt to define the complex parameters of a post-colonial discourse and its relationship to the narrative of migration and exile.

Naipaul is a thorough colonial as he was born a colonial in 1932, almost 30 years before independence. He comes to terms with the fantasy of the idea of England and the equally potent idea of India. He is out to evolve an alternative vision, an aesthetic which could move beyond the reductive oppositions of a colonial consciousness, the crisis of a dying colonialism which gave birth to the narrative of nationalism. The authority of the hegemonic myths of empire began to be displaced by the evolution of a cultural grammar that questioned the epistemological bases of a received history. All this gave enormous potential to a creative writer to experiment with a new narrative forms. Thus they came in the process of redefining the colonial past and develop the sense of belonging. Precisely Naipaul's writings comprise both colonial and post-colonial consciousness.

He is trapped in a dream of wholeness and fulfilment both as colonial attempting to assimilate into the English conon or as the Diasporic Asiatic (attempting to return to the lost homeland), both as tainted detached Brahmin and exiled colonial Anglophile. His exile consciousness, in which the memory of home becomes paramount in narratives whose home itself is but a memory, differs considerably from the modern such as Joyce, Conard, or Eliot. The East Indian presence in the Caribbean islands is a historical process known as 'second system of slavery' or 'coolie odyssey', the post modern phase of Indian Diaspora also called 'jahaji'-bhai' or 'Black Atlantic'. For a large population the Caribbean land becomes the land of no return and the question of nativity and homeland emerged and talked in most of the creative writing. The world of Naipaul is full of such characters and climate. *The Mystic Masseur* (1957), *Miguel Street* (1959), *The Suffrage of Elvira* (1958), *A House for Mr. Biswas* (1961), *In a Free State* (1971), *Guerrillas* (1975) and *A Bend in the River*(1979) are a few works which may be cited as works of true Diasporic consciousness.

Biswas is a typical Naipaulian character and Tulsis build their world to preserve the past; it is the lost world of India which represents the nostalgic desire. Symbolic representation acquaints us with the ulterior motive of the writer. Hanuman House represents Biswas's life built on shaky foundations, constantly shifting and shored up by the perpetual; enactment and performance of ancient rituals as fragments to replace the original desire. Here Tulsi household aspires to the los condition of India replacing a space where centres and peripheries, motherland and Diasporas enter into the relationships of mutual reinforcement and uncanny displacement. The entire novel; is a literal search for home and it is nothing but mounting demand of a centre within the society which may be a makeshift but would be a place to dictate from. When Biswas gets a roof over his head we find Naipaul's own displacement living in a solitary attic room in Streatham Hill.

It is all about Naipaul himself, a period of anxiety and destitution with penniless pocket, and the state of homelessness. The experience was so bitter that he did not read the novel himself for subsequent twenty years.

Landeg White in his book *'V.S.Naipaul: A Critical Introduction* (London: Macmillan, 1975, 8) says that after writing *A House for Mr.Biswas* Naipaul becomes "a man threatened by desolation, driven within himself, reduced to homelessness". He grows resentful of Trinidad and in *The Middle Passage* (1962) he describes it as "unimportant, uncreative, cynical—a society which denied itself heroes." He is disenchanted with the life of India, its realities strike him like England. In *An Area of Darkness* (1964) his India is an untainted world of imagination in childhood and he comes across with the wider dimensions of his Diasporic inheritance, the fear of being lost in translation for ever, 'faceless' at the Churchgate Station, 'sink without a trace'. Even the escape to London was illusionary, *An Area of Darkness* has the intense sense of cultural displacement that refers to his life in London and his search for ancestral home in India; heb refers India as 'resting place for the imagination'. *The Mimic Men* (1967) is also a novel of exile, the experience of being immigrant in Britain that we find later in *The Enigma of Arrival* (1987), the true potential of the crosscultural material. As a writer he was in search of raw material fir his writings in the London of the fifties, linguistic notion of Englishness and immigrant tenants of the self. In this context, it is pertinent to cite Stuart Hall who defines cultural identity as that which:

> ... come from somewhere, have histories. But like everything which is historical, they undergo constant transformation. (213)

Michael Ondaatjee in his book *Running in the Family* gives a different dimension:

> Everyone was vaguely related and had Sinhalese, Tamil, Dutch British and Burgher blood in them going back to many generations—My father always claimed to be a Ceylon Tamil, though that was probably more valid about three centuries earlier—however, when he was asked by one of the British governors what his nationality was, he said, 'God alone knows, your excellency. (41)

Naipaul analyses N.C. Chaudhuri's *The Autobiography of an Unknown Citizen* in a different way when he says that the achievement of *Autobiography* "contained within itself both India and the West—no better account of the penetration of Indian mind by the West—and, by extension, of the penetration of one culture by another—will be or can now be written". (Naipaul, 1976, 64)

He does not find a neglect of the immediate environment which was so intensely felt in his reading of Mahatma Gandhi's autobiography. His own personality and character is moulded by the influence of various environments and a good account of his earlier life can be found in the Prologue to an *Autobiography in Finding the Centre*. He was lost in the crowd of chaos of his big joint family. Later on Port of Spain became his colonial home but shift on the intellectual place as well as that of cultural continued, distancing him from the native civilization with uncomfortable displacement. Surprisingly, while Chaudhuri believes that redemption lies in movement towards the West Naipaul's preoccupation is in 'finding a centre'; a decentralized world and the desire to breakdown stereotypes of personal identity do not hold any charm for him. Chaudhuri's dictum is "Always go West" and he has followed it in his personal life. Shashi Tharoor is of the view that he has carried the Macaulayan fantasy to its absurd extreme.

Naipaul's writings have the West-centric mode of analysis. *An Area of Darkness* which comes out of his first visit to India presents a gloomy picture of India, an exhausted and feeble India under Nehru. He finds Nuhruvian idealism a failure, and this is gauged by the Western standards. He castigates everything Indian as 'mimicry' of the West. For him the colonial

India and the colonial Trinidad are similar. Yet he is disgusted with the bureaucratic set up, the behaviour of a common man, and the ritual obsessions of India.

Khushwant Singh, who personally took Naipaul around for sight seeing during the latter's visit to India has noted in his autobiography *Truth, Love and Little Malice* that Naipaul seemed to be obsessed with the faith and squalor of India than the pleasant sights it had to offer (393). Consequently his response is on of immediate disgust and fear, and an urge to escape from the maddening scenario. Like Paul Scott who visited India and found all out of tune, Naipaul, too, finds his inflated dreams of the land of ancestors is shattered and says, "India must progress, must stamp out corruption, must catch up with the west". K.N. Daruwalla says, "Naipaul is like a mother bird rummaging in the nest of doubts" (107). This is how the concept of identities, homeland and nationalism are constructed: identities as vacillating identities incorporating multivalent elements in its making, situating not within Bhabha's 'third space', homeland as a target of continuous search and movement, and nationality the rational construct out of irrational approach whether historical or intellectual. Such writers structure their works around memory, an essential ingredient in the making of a nation and national identity.

Through his various characters Naipaul interrogates, subverts, and translates those areas of the immigrant imaginary previously bound by the discursive world of English letters of an imperial history where post-colonial 'action' is quoted as 'reaction' to a specific cultural void, to replace the 'sense of missing' not as a 'creative intervention', 'transformation' or 'writing back' (Helen Tiffin), or 'semiotics of resistance'. *An Area of Darkness* also expresses his fear of extinction as he says, "I had been made in Trinidad and England; recognition of my difference was necessary to me—to be a colonial was to know a certain kind of security but one has to abandon that fixed world, it was necessary to lose one's preoccupations of what the novel should do for the romantic fantasy of England as a purely literary region untrammelled by the accidents of history or background". In conversations with Stephen Schiff Naipaul admits, "Narrative occurs all the time— your coming here is a narrative—It's all narrative, but it's a matter of choosing. It's when you're doing the other kind of writing—you start looking for a thing called plot and you get into trouble—Narrative is something large going on around you all the time—Plot assumes that the world has been explored—Whereas I am still exploring the world. I don't know the world yet. And there is narrative there, in every explanation. The writers of plots know the world—I began to understand that quite late."(148)

He was a disillusioned member of Caribbean Artist's Movement and his actual experience of Oxford turned out to be a mockery of his expectations because he "sought continuously to relate literature to life". In George Lamming's *The Pleasure of Exile* we have the construction of the colonial idea of England based on tyranny indoctrinated by the intricacy of the discursive world represented by Prospero's 'texts', yet the gap between literature and life, a world and a society, founded precariously in imagination, but rooted in a different and alien cultural context portray Naipaul's making as a writer of Diaspora and that of a post-colonial era.

Naipaul's exile has its own pain and pleasure but he gets recognition with knowledge that the vision of English literature is alien and has diminished his own, misread as mimicry, not able to perceive his difference through the performative and potentially liberating elements of his colonial background. In his first three books set in Trinidad—*The Mystic Masseur, The Saiffrage of Elvira* and *Miguel Street* he is satiric of the illiteracy, disordered and anarchic lives of the East Indians and has a sense of oddity of the people, for example, Ganesh of *The Mystic Masseur* is targeted for his ambitions to be a fraudulent masseur, a pundit and later politician, above all, it is history of our times and it reveals his being contemptuous of what he loved and feared too. *In Finding the Centre* (1984) he has to locate himself and in *Miguel Street*, his boys are translated from the mock-heroic calypsonian street world of Port of Spain to the underworld in *The Lovely Londoners*, a model from home, his father's persistence in the writing of *Gurudeva and Other Tales,* stories written from within a community.

Naipaul's understanding of his Diasporic inheritance facilitates the process of making and remaking of his Diasporic past of cultural and historical displacement as well as imaginative reconstruction of identity through a process of symbolic and aesthetic renewal, negotiated and refigured as one of his characters in *A Bend in the River* says,' home was hardly a place I could turn to. Home was something in my head. It was something I had lost.'

Diaspora and Diasporic literature is about exile, that is, separation from one's homeland and about migration, transformation and constant renewal; this home is not an object of geographical quest but the fulfilment of the need to belong and a deep undefinable need, the 'connections' and 'continuity' of life.

Works Cited

Damian, Grant, *Salman Rushdie*, Plymouth: Northcote House, 1999.

Daruwalla, K.N., "The Wounded Continent and Nirad Babu and Naipaul" in Swapan Gupta, Ed., *Nirad C. Chaudhri, The First Hundered Years: A Celebration,* New Delhi: Harper Collins, 1997.

Ghosh, Amitav, *The Hungry Tide*, New Delhi: Harper Collins, 2004.

_______ *The Shadow Lines,* Delhi: Ravi Dayal Pub., 1998.

Hall, Stuart, "Cultural Identity and Diaspora", in Patrick Williams and Laura Chrisman (eds.), *Colonial Discourse and Post colonial Theory: A Reader,* London: Whaeatsheaf.

Hamilton, I., The First Life of Salman Rushdie, in *The New Yorker*, Dec. 1995.

Maini, D.S., "The Complex Fate of V.S. Naipaul", *Colonial Consciousness in Commonwealth Literature: Essays Presented to Prof. C.D. Narsimhaiah*, (Ed.) G.S. Amur and S.K. Desai, Bombay: Smaiya, 1984.

Mathur, O.P., 'The Rhetoric of Horror in Rushdie's *Shame*', *Indian Writing in English: Critical Appraisals*, (Ed.), A.N. Prasad, New Delhi: Sarup and Sons, 2005.

Mukherjee, B., *Darkness,* Harmondsworth : Penguin, 1985.

Naik, M.K., & Narayan, S.A., (Ed.), *Indian English Fiction: A Critical Study*, New Delhi: Pencraft International, 2009.

_______ *A History of Indian English Literature*, New Delhi: Sahitya Akademi, 1999.

Naipaul, V.S., *The Return of Eva Peron with the Killings in Trinidad,* Harmondsworth: Penguin, 1983.

_______*An Area of Darkness*, London: Andre Deutsch, 1964.

_______*India: A Wounded Civilization*, Harmondsworth: Penguin, 1979.

_______*India: A Million Mutinies Now,* London: Vintage Paperbacks, 1998.

_______*The Middle Passage*, Harmondsworth: Penguin, 1969.

_______*The Overcrowded Barracoon and Other Articles*, London: Andre Deutsch, 1972.

_______*Writing in Limbo*, New York: Cornell Univ. Press, 1992.

Nasrin, Taslima, *Lajja*, Penguin Books, 1993.

Ondaatjee, Michael, *Running in the Family,* London: Picador, 1982

Raman, E., "What is a Nation", *Nation and Narration*, (Ed.). Homi K. Bhabha, London: Routledge, 1990.

Rosalind, A., "Chutnification of History : Indian Reality in *Midnight's Children*", *The Expatriate Indian Writing in English*, Vol.2 (Ed.), Vinoda & Sailaja, New Delhi: Prestige Books, 2006.

Rushdie, Salman, *Midnight's Children,* London: Picador, 1982.

_______*Imaginary Homelands,* London: Granta, 1992.

_______*East West,* London: Cape, 1994.

_______"The Indian Writer in England", *The Eye of the Beholder: Indian Writing in English,* (Ed.) Maggie Butcher, London: Commonwealth Institute, 1983.

Said, E., *Reflections on Exile,* U.K. Granta; India:Penguin, 2001.

Singh, Khushwant, *Truth, Love and Little Malice: An Autobiography*, New Delhi: Penguin, 2003.

Stuart, Hall, David Held and Tony McGrew, (eds.), *Modernity and its Features*, Cambridge: Polity Press/Open University, 1992.

20.Usha, D.R., "Problematizing Perception: Amitav Ghosh's The Shadow Lines", *The Expatriate Writing in English,* (Ed.), T. Vinoda & P.Saijala, New Delhi: Prestige Pub., 2006.

Vinoda & Shailja, *The Expatriate Indian Writing in English*, Prestige Pub., New Delhi, 2006.

Walsh, William, "India and the Novel," *The Pelican Guide to English Literature* (Ed.) Boris Ford, Vol. 8, Harmondsworth: Penguin, 1983.

3

Pattern in the Type of Characters

In simple words, the characters of Diaspora writings speak a lot of colonial, post-colonial and the world of exile. Be it Amitav Ghosh, Salman Rushdie, Shashi Tharoor, Bharati Mukherjee, Gita Mehta, Anita Desai, Rohinton Mistry, Anurag Mathur, Meera Syal, Jhumpa Lahiri, or anyone else. Their lifestyle, conversation, body language, aspirations and pursuit speak volumes and this chapter of study is devoted to the same sort of exploration.

In the Diasporic writings, we can detect subaltern voice, alien pang, feministic cry, repressed utterances, desperate discriminatory articulations, anxious helpless pronouncements, etc. All assume the proportion of a categorical articulation but nothing disheartening—rather a cry of survival and sensibility. Here Edward Said's *Culture and Imperialism* becomes relevant which says, "Survival, in fact, is about the connections between things"; in Eliot's phrase, reality cannot be deprived of the "other echoes that inhabit the garden" (336).

Let us take Gita Mehta, as our first Diaspora writer, who came in prominence with *Karma Cola* which interprets India to the Western world and it becomes accessible to the diverse audience as a story of her homeland. Through her eyes, one can see the "indigenous traditions, folklore, cultural values and practices"—a country which is ethnically, geographically and religiously diverse—its tension and contradiction, sophistication and collision, reconciliations and variations, perennial and metaphysical.

'India' has been the sole interest for the Indian Diaspora and Gita Mehta is one of them. She begins with *Karma Cola*, lingers over *A River Sutra* and concludes in *Snakes and Ladders*. The present paper seeks to examine Gita Mehta's endeavour to present her native place India in "glacial progress towards liberation; more than the political freedom", the modern India: beyond comprehension—to be marvelled upon, with specific case of *Snakes and Ladders*, a non-fiction.

Snakes and Ladders happens to be a collection of her brilliant essays on modern India which are at once fragmentary and personal, as she herself admits in the *Foreword* of the book. The game of 'Snakes and Ladders' is primarily the 'Game of Knowledge' used by the author as a metaphor for 'a meditation on humanity's progress towards liberation', for the 'roller-coaster ride' after Independence, the 'highs so sudden we have become light-headed with exhilaration, the laws too deep to even contemplate solution'; it illustrates our attempts to move our ancient civilization towards modern enlightenment. The author feels that we have vaulted our painful stages of bitter experience, as felt by other countries, as if lifted by ladders we had no right to expect; at the same time, the snakes of the past nightmares swallowed us back to square one.

In the first chapter 'Freedom's Song' she talks of her birth and the role of her parents in bringing her up and their roles in the Freedom Struggle of India; her house as 'Absconder's Paradise', complimented by the Vicereine of India, later imprisonment and the humiliating experience at the hands of the Britishers during the nationalistic movement which had broken the *shibboleths* that constrained the conventional Indian society, yet they could discover their own strength in doing so. Whatever the case may be the author says repeatedly, "This is my damned soil", and quotes the words of her uncle, "I wouldn't recommend my life to everyone. But I think when you face everyday for years, and are lucky enough to survive, you learn a little about its limits"(12). She recalls Sarojini Naidu as her mentor who used to call Mahatma Gandhi a 'Mickey Mouse' and Robert Payne who used to call Naidu as 'exuberant, earthy, irreverent, improbable,—one of those robust personality of such woman is 'fearlessness' and she says, "Their courage did not seem to be inspired by self-aggrandisement or ideological dogma or religious fervour—those certainties which usually fuel suicidal actions—and sometimes I wonder if they indeed possess what Mahatma Gandhi called a kind of moral force."(11)

In Independent India, the things have changed fast: "from individual fearlessness in the face of social and political injustice to craven courting of those who possess social and political power" (12). Such is her memory of a senior bureaucrat with a genuine conviction that Mrs. Gandhi's family owned India. Mrs. Gandhi was observed with an imagined inheritance which breed intense paranoia about those who refuse to accept it, it also brought spy-versus-spy paraphernalia of the world be despot. Yet it was her 'dammed soil.' She faces the question: "Why does no one want to be an Indian?" The question may be innocent but it shows a sort of racial insult to which her reply is, "I suppose, some of us have it thrust upon us" (14). As a child she thought of getting respect for the richness of the past, but she failed to garner reverence on that ground because, the grim figures of the present where the realities of youth, "a burden of social and economic disparities which even the most Herculean endeavour seemed powerless to reverse" (16). The only reaction was: "What have you got but snakes and monkeys? Indians are just poor and dirty and backward!" (15). She could mutter 'damned, unfair' (16). To the 'self-confident dwarfs from the first world' (16). Another important reason that the author diagnoses is "to be an Indian today is to be assaulted by the enormity of the tasks we have inherited with freedom" (16). This task is targeted at illiteracy, poverty, corruption and the incomprehensible democracy.

In the section 'My Damned Soil' Gita Mehta describes the contradictory realities of India, its concept of nation and national integration, the annoying absence of identity, lack of homogeneity and the diversity in its vicious forms : language, religion, region, etc. which attracts comments from different corners of different sorts, such as:

> Those who believe in the dialectics of materialism or the authority of history wander through the ruins of glorious empires and tell us India has burned nothing from the past. Others play statistical roulette and tell us India has no future. (20)

Then we have some catchy accurate phrase, for instance, India as 'functioning anarchy', 'the sum of a million worlds enclosed by oceans an three sides, the mighty Himalayas on the north,' 'the land of fabulous contrast', 'the degrees to which diversity is attained, unity retained' (Arnold's definition of civilization, adequate for India), etc. The writer is assured that "Indian culture is still in business that Krishna will continue to play his flute whether he is in a field, Rolls, or a rocket" (24). It is in India only that "we are still faced to remember that people are individuals as well as anthropological or economic statistics"; (25) and yet "we could never survive as democracy because a hungry man can have no understanding of freedom... people whose stomachs are empty have no idea what democracy means"; (29) "...the diversities of India's past are more than matched by the immense complicities of her present, her problems infinitely more complicated than the simplistic solutions offered either by her own leaders or by experts from abroad" (30), and finally, 'India progresses, a monumental juggernaut of contradictory realities' (30); and say "That is Bharat. That is India." (31)

The second section of the book is rather stereotyped where the titles are self-suggestive such as 'Banish Poverty' and Banish Charity'. In 'Reinventing the Wheel' she talks of the art of wavering, the fabric and machination of Indian culture. In "Food for Thought" there is a minute description of the famine in Maharastra in 1973, the policy of Pt. Nehru and Shastri and the beginning of Green Revolution. By 1980 the things were completely changed, farmers going on nationwide movements, demanding higher prices for their crops, demand for tax concession and subsidies, etc. But the result was not a happy one: "like her landless labourers India was herself now in bondage, facing ever larger interest payments to her foreign creditors on ever larger loans. But her peasants, her migrant workers, her craftsmen dependent on diminishing village patronage, were still leaving the land."(63)

Gita Mehta says that the old India was poor in which "self-denial was solidarity" (65), and around Independence we were influenced by Gandhi's austerity which Sarojini Naidu observed as "costing Indians a lot to keep Gandhi poor" (66), a sagacious comment at the murky economy. The author recalls her early days of sixties: "we were living in the age of ideology, the very heart of a Cold War that pitted social justice against ruthless capitalism, and we were our poverty with pride ... . After all, it was the heyday of Nehru's socialism" (67). Later on, the steps taken by Mrs. Gandhi was for "self reliance, independence from the Western commercial imperialism that had replaced the Western political imperialism" (68) then came Rajiv Gandhi who dismissed hollow self-reliance and opened India's economy to the world, deregulating industry, slashing taxes. But his love for foreign goods in all ways could only make possible: "Homespun was out, luxury goods were in" (69), and for the independent India "it was politically correct to be rich". (69)

India kept on changing its hue and colour; in the seventies it attracted foreigners for 'spiritual enlightenment' and in the eighties, with Rajiv Gandhi as Prime Minister, Indian economy underwent liberalization and "money became the new enlightenment" (70). At the same time, this was the time when the author could feel "more patriotism paled into insignificance" (71) when she was invited to address "five hundred international young Presidents and their wives arriving for India 1986". The self-confidence of Indians got strength in the eighties: "The skills of the modern world are by no means alien to us. Doctors, engineers, laboratory workers, economists, accountants—at the level of medium technology, Indians are second to none. And each time there is a new advance in technology, Indians are ready to seize it" (85-86). Yet we are different from the West: "Ancient pragmatisms are India's saving grace, preserving a way of life in which the machine is still used by man, not one in which man becomes the machine. But that is a difficult thing to someone from the West" (85).

If Malaysia, South Korea, Singapore, Thailand and Indonesia are known as South East Asian Tigers, India is the Caged Tiger. "One Indian Prime Minister after another, in the attempt to remove poverty, had only mired us further in poverty"(87).

The author has an accurate calculation: in the fifties Nehru's dream of self-sufficient economy through rapid industrialization, neglected the needs of rural India; the sixties had green revolution; the seventies had obsessive centralization and spiralling farm subsidies: in the eighties Rajiv Gandhi's interest in a new India was soon exchanged for the political manoeuvrings of the old India and his successor V. P. Singh was less concerned with economic development than with political change; in the nineties our foreign currency reserves were depleted and nation's gold was sent to London as surety against the international loans; in 1991 Narshimha Rao moved from Indian socialism to market economy—and this India goes on, there is nothing to stop us; but democracy is a time-bomb and we are in a land of million mutinies, as V. S. Naipaul says.

Gita Mehta recalls Dr. Ambedkar who drafted constitution and had cautioned against hero-worship in democracy; it is dangerous with powers which enable him to subvert this institution of democracy. Perhaps the author's final pronouncement is remarkable when she says, "For sheer idiosyncratic panache the spectacle of Indian democracy is unique'. (94) and the most annoying statement, "Modern India is a fiction."(95)

The gist of the whole book *Snakes and Ladders: A View of Modern India* is to be found in the last chapter of the second section of the book titled 'Manogement of Crisis' where she says, 'India is a fiction—a fiction in search of an administration'(97). We have the vision of our old generation, that of, freedom, equality and non-violence which have turned into siren songs which N.C. Chaudhuri calls 'Continent of Circe' and calls India her political seduction have truly made swine out of men and women; "it's scale of India"(97). Surprisingly Indian political leaders are finding tea and monarchy more palatable than governance; the reflected power creates megalomania in elected representative; democracy demands accountability which melts in the crowds. India is changing fast and in such a case megalomaniac is a convenient retreat; it is politics partially; but we are not ready to endure the injustice of the past. Economically we are yet to find a system of development for the vociferous population and the world of exploding scientific and financial expansion bringing out inimitable chaos. In this world winning an election is tantamount to winning a lottery and it makes the political corruption endemic, pilloried by satirists, yet from the vantage of time we are leading towards the unknown with Ambedkar's constitutional dreams and incorruptible non-violent politics of Gandhi.

The third section of the book starts with the sudden death /murder of Gandhi by a Hindu fanatic as he was preparing to leave on a peace march for the killing fields of Partition, the mass exodus, fleeing the orgy of fear and savagery, for whom non-violence and proud humility went hand in hand, and who believed that Indians would govern themselves with greater justice than their colonial masters. However, India has seen the beginning of nepotism with Pt. Nehru as anointed leader of the Indian National Congress by his own father while travelling to a nationalist convention in 1929, and later Pt. Nehru appointing his daughter Indira Gandhi as President of the party organization, both of them becoming the Prime Minister of the country subsequently, leading to the shut down of democracy in the whole of India, for instance, the dismissal of the Communist government in Kerala in 1959; this was the first major act of corruption in free India's public life, denouncing the left claim that communism was a legitimate road to social justice.

The post-Independence India started with Congress culture and the Congressmen who cynically retained power by playing on the fears of the country's minorities: the Muslims, the lower castes, the Buddhists, the Christians, etc. The author recalls her visit to the North East (Assam) in 1978 when the turmoil was at its peak and there was a movement against the people of other states residing in Assam, they were brutally beat and compelled to leave the state; India's pluralism and Gandhi's non-violence were at stake; the chaos and crisis need no rehearsal and it was in full swing.

Non-violence is India's creed but it has failed enormously. Now the horrified Indians could watch in disbelief as our politicians forged ever more unholy alliances to keep themselves in power and it resulted in exponential growth of corruption in public life, dependence criminals to ensure electoral success, increasing hatred as pattern of democracy, etc.

India has seen its dark days of the emergency of 1975 and the excesses of the period, resulting in Mrs. Gandhi's loosing her parliamentary seat by a massive margin; the Emergency was India's watershed. Another watersheds could be sensed in the Sikh resolution, the Blue Star Operation, the murder of Mrs. Gandhi and the upheavals afterwards and the author is surprised to articulate "The wonder is that India still exists to surmount them ... Democracy of India is a wonder of the world ... and its guardian is not the politician so beloved of feature writers but the faceless, nameless, all enduring Indian voters" (159). The problems that we have to face are sectarianism, affirmative action, political assassination, Civil War, unstable coalitions, the electronic marketing of political aspirants, separatism, corruption, and above all, the rhetoric of religious hatred as an illegal use of political process.

In the fourth section of the book Gita Mehta begins with defining India and she cites the definitions of Mark Twain and Alex Aronson. Mark Twain visited India at the end of the nineteenth century and wrote of his delirium, "...the land of dreams and romance, of fabulous poverty, of splendour and rags, of places and hovels, of famine and pestilence, of genii and giants and Alladin lamps, of tigers and elephants, of cobra and the jungle, the country of a hundred nations and hundred tongues, of a thousand religions and two million gods, cradle of humane race, birth place of human speech, mother of history, grandmother of legend, great grandmother of tradition, whose yesterdays bear date with the mouldering antiquities of the rest of the nations—the sole country under the sun that is endowed with imperishable interest for alien peasant, for lettered and ignorant, wise and fool, rich and poor, bond and free, the one land all men desire to see, and having seen once, by even a glimpse, would not give the glimpse for the shows of all the rest of the globe combined."

On the other hand, Alex Aronson said that India was a civilization and "civilization is always a process: not a being but a becoming"(164). However Gita Mehta has her own influences/ observations that labels India as "Karma Bhumi and Land of Experience" (164). Even today these observations are astute with unpredictable and surprising civilization defying definition of any sort, may be due to her indolence. The author is of the view that, "In any case, in a world of perpetual motion India remains a perpetual becoming, a vast and protean sea of human improvisations on the great dance of time' (164). She further admits, "The art if there is one in India, is supposed to lie in the living"(175). Therefore, she writes about filming (Satyajit Ray), the telecommunications company, the relevance and significance of trees and forests, love songs of India (Jaydeva's *Gita Govinda*), the greatest sages of India, the national anthem and the final acknowledgement to God for His fabulous gift of making 'India at his leisure'.

Obviously, India remains an undefined entity, God's special gift to mankind and despite all its distractions and drawbacks, 'a thing of beauty, a joy forever'; like V. S. Naipaul she does not have a negative proposition as 'an area of darkness', 'a wounded civilization' or 'a million mutinies' rather India as 'Karma Bhumi'—the land of Experience—dismissing other countries as the "land of consumers"(199), "an extraordinary world spinning through an extraordinary time". (VIII)

Indian Diaspora writing reveals an unbelievable fact that the crowd of characters has a pattern, in this way or that way, which can be easily identified while going through the works of different writers. In fact, Indian Diaspora writing got into prominence with Salman Rushdie's *'Midnight's Children'* and the protagonist of the novel Saleem Sinai is victim of absurdity, which he himself confesses. Rushdie presents a double narrative here, available in his journey from Kashmir to Bombay as a historical imperative intertwined with the ingredients of his own life, flourishing the saga of partition. Absurdity reigns supreme in the novel, right from the presentations of the actions of Adam Aziz, the grandfather of Saleem Sinai, who is unceremoniously unghosted for venturing to use the perforated sheet as a disguise for ghost.

Rushdie moves with history as he begins in the part with the arrival of Adam Aziz in his home in Kashmir which is primitive but picturesque. Adam Aziz has a tall figure and appears to be robust and energetic with a face that may be termed as resplendent and nose of historical dominances, the basis of so many explanations in the novel. This extraordinary nose of Aziz is a matter of interest in the novel, to many people it means many things; the German Else believed it was a nose which could use as a bridge to cross a river, the old scrofulous Tai insisted it was a nose on which could be founded future dynasties, an envy to all the past emperors etc. - to through this interesting nose Aziz inter the plot of the novel, the world of Museum Ghani, the land owner's daughter. He was seduced by Naseem and fell into obsession for marriage with his daughter.

It is disgusting to note while Finnah has created for himself a whole new nation, India has created a unique race of children learn in learn in that metaphorical hour of midnight, the "children of the time-fathered—by history.... In a country which is itself a sort of dream" (118). The temporal symbol of midnight gives to the narrative a timeless dimensions, reinforced by dreams and nightmares, psychological journeys, hieroglyphic images and archetypal characters- which finally gives birth to the narrator Saleem Sinai at the midnight, the precise hair of attraction, the momentous hair.

Saleem Sinai is a changeling, a victim of Mary Pereira's ultimate act of love and devotion to her nation loving, British-hating lover Joseph. Sinai has methwoldian blue eyes with the same sort of nose of his grandfather, call it Erench nose. He is born of a doomed Vanita in a riot of colours, in the historical hour of Independence when it. Nehru was making historical speech in parliament, there was jubilations in the street and there was a dream of new India. It was the hour of junction of dream and reality, history and nightmare, and Sinai was a part of the race midnight's children, synonymous with the birth of a nation.

This is 'human- interest drama', and the magic hour of history is "are fleeting instant in the Age of Darkness, Kali

Yuga in which the caw of morality has been reduced to standing, tectningly on a single leg" (194). On the other hand, the narrative has other version of history which began on Friday, February 18, 3012 BC, the date which declares the death of the 'eternal love God Krishna' and marked the beginning of the Age of Darkness, the Kali Yuga, "the age when property gives a man rank, when wealth is equated with virtue, when passion becomes the sole band between men and women, when falsehood brings success" (194). A reader is guided by the narrator and then appears Padma, "the lotus goddess, the one who possesses Dung—the lotus calyx which grew out of Vishnu's navel—Padmath source, the mother of time" (194-95). This Padma is also the beloved of Vanita's son Shiva who was changed into Saleem Sinai and who later on became the hero of Bangaladesh war. Finally Padma is merely an omnipresent voice of the narrator's insidious impression of his present, juxtaposed on his irretrievable part. Saleem Sinai is the important lover of Padma who marries Parvati, the witch who is carrying the bastard child of Shiva her merciless lover. Shiva is Saleem Sinai and Saleem Sinai is Shiva in an interchangeable confession of identities, the antithesis of choice had come to rule of his life. This novel is a maze of characters which are mixed with events and strung in calendars. Rushdie wants to create a world of his own choice; he wants to define it and so the characters do not seem to be fictional, they are out of the absurdities of Saleem, rather symbols used to modify history and there is resurgence of links that clasp together the chain of events, and the events can be linked symbols.

Precisely, *Midnight's Children* conceptualizes a period of about 63 years of India's pre- and post-colonial twentieth century history dealing with the major events of Independence, partition, etc. encapsulating the experience of three generations of the Sinai family and their experience of Srinagar, Amritsar, Agra, Bombay and Karachi; Rushdie provides us the taste of History through the experience of Saleem's pickle factory in the day and recording of the experience in right, he says, "one day perhaps, the world may taste the pickle of history" (461). It begins with Independence, the midnight of 14-15 August 1947, of course, retrospectively; it progresses in a cynical way and with a cyclic and regenerative time having an open-ending. It is tripartite in structure, presenting a cross-section of humanity of Indians, Muslims and Anglo Indians—beginning with Jallianwallah Bagh, Indo-Pakistan war of 1963 and ending in the emergency of 1977.

The colonizer and the colonized are placed face to face; this the order of Brigadier Dyer to open fire on a political demonstration in Jallianwallah Bagh and thousand of Indian killed is viewed by the colonizer to bring order to choose where as the colonized view it as a cold blooded massacre of innocents; Adam Aziz considers it unprovoked killing and Dyer finds it 'jolly good thing'.

It is a historical fact and truth which Rushdie calls "ambiguous for Rushdie reality is built on our prejudices, misconceptions, ignorance, perceptiveness and knowledge" (1992, 25).

Sinai's birth coincides with the birth of a nation and the phenomenon of the great divide between the colonial and Independent India; it is also symptomatic of Sinai's identity crisis, a divided character, the element of instability; though Saleem means 'simple' and 'straightforward' Sinai means 'sin the moon' so his life is bound to be troublesome.

Critics find Saleem Sinai synonymous to India; Saleem Sinai is India in miniature: the disfiguring birthmarks as the holocaust of the partitions, the bulbous 'Byzantine dames' of the temples suggestive of the Himalayas and the ice like eccentricity of his sky blue eyes as the azure skies of Kashmir; in the same way the dark stains, the western hairline and the dark patches colouring the eastern ears stand for the two wings of Pakistan, and the depression of the chin is like the thinness of the southern part of the Indian peninsula. The most marked feature of Saleem's physiognomy is his long nose which is indicative of India's pride and self-glorification which is valuable during Chinese aggression, Bangladesh war, etc. He is the most sensitive character in both physical and moral dimensions having extraordinary power of smell and sensing. He combines individually subjective with the supra-individually objective that is, the family history with that of the sub-continent.

Rushdie is prompted by the disposition of the Indian mind to see correspondence in seemingly unrelated events; consequently, every event has both individual and historical meaning, for instance, Saleem's grandparents stopover in Amritsar on their way from Kashmir to Agra to experience the Jallianwallah Bagh massacre and finds his wife different from her profile of being orthodox, family centered and strong willed, the marriage of Saleem's parents on the day the first atom bomb exploded in 1947 to destroy thousands and to usher in the nuclear age, their departure from Bombay on the day of partition and the announcement of the day of Independence, that is, on the 4 June 1947, the acquisition of their own house on 15 August 1947 and the birth of Saleem from the Englishman Mr. Methwold. In the same way, Saleem's grandfather returns to Kashmir on the day in December 1963 when the hair of prophet Mahamed is stolen from the shrine of Hazarat Bal mosque in Srinagar on 23 Sept. 1965; Saleem's family is killed and the India's air force strafes Rawalpindi; the narrator's powerful adversary Shiva moves in with Parvati, the witch in May 1974 when India explodes its first nuclear test bomb in Rajasthan; the birth of Adam on 25 June 1975 when the emergency was clamped—all these instance suffice the belief that Saleem and India are correlated both literally and metaphorically.

Rushdie has presented Saleem as a critical historian of India; in fact Saleem is Rushdie himself in delimiting the part, the tradition and the democracy—all shaping the present. One has to acknowledge the contribution of the great masters/makers of the denting of the nation and affirm the creative power of the imagination to construct reality and a true narrative. The evolution of Mian Abdullah, the creation of free Island convocation opposed to the Muslim league which demanded separate Muslim state, the murder of Mian Abdullah at the hands of league, the appearance of picture Singh, the snake charmer and leader of the magicians ghetto bringing back the hope of a religiously and socially heterogeneous society of India—all fellow historical pattern. Saleem Sinai follows the vision of Mian Abdullah and in picture Singh he finds the future of India and its possibilities which may bring an end to religious factionalism, dynastic rule and cultural differences. Saleem recognizes the diversity of Indias population and his utterance is significant, "To understand just one life, you have to swallow the whole world" (126). He avoids Gandhi, only touches Nehru- Gandhi family and dwell on the common people, their wonderful language and idiosyncratic locations, such as, Tai, the boatman, his own grandmother, etc.

The Bangladesh war is filtered through the experience of Ayooba, Shaheed, Farooq and Saleem. Evidently the everyday experience of the average people matter most. Padma is a co-creator and critic of the narrative representing the Indian masses, representing the Indian masses with their down-to-earth reality, emphasizing on base material, that is, earth, transformational phase and aesthetic incarnation or form—they all constitute reality. Padma's role is crucial as it helps Saleem to confront multidimensional reality; they form feminine-masculine polarity and Hindu-Muslim cultural polarity. It also helps the genuine theme of the navel to evolve the duality of all reality as Saleem-Shiva motif, highlighting the split in the educated Indian's orientation to life where Western influences play a vital role. Saleem is torm between the ancient oriental would view and the clock-ridden would. Tai represents the ancient oriental would and Shiva the clock-ridden. Adam Aziz forfeits Tai's ageless organize cosmos. Aziz is Saleem's grandfather whose Western education has taken away his 'faith' and fractured his vision; he has dubious belief in history and material science and is septic about God, which is why Saleem has inherited fractured belief, and his destiny bows to 'women and history' when he says 'women have made me; and also unmade' (483). It reveals Rushdie's experience of 'too many women' as "the dynamic aspect of maga, as cosmic energy, which is represented as the female organ"(485). Saleem's treatment of Mary, Mumtaz and vanita shows their weakness and at the end of the day he gains strength, understanding and belief from Padma.

Rushdie makes the image of mother complicated and so his concept of Bharat Mata is, and so is the image of Kali, the destructive mother and so stands India to him—mother of ambiguity, orthodoxy, superstition, etc.—this shapes the belief of Saleem and the theme of the novel as a whole.

A comic vision is displayed in respect for 'many' position and power in the post-Independence India and the characters go for it, for instance, Adam Sinai's false Oxford drawal and bottles of gin, Lilia Sabarmati's pianola and Saleem's masquerades—and above all, in the speech pattern of urban Indian population. The post-Independence India has the colonial hang over explicit in speech pattern and this is seen in the language of urban population most and the characters of the novel carry it, later on it became part of the Indian language which Rushdie calls 'Chutneyfied English'. The growth and development of free India is reflected in the growth and development of Saleem, who represents the intellectual and imagination Indian who can think, feel and communicate with others, who can host diverse viewpoints and who has deep interest in the people around him. He has sound moral values which bring about hatred for fanaticism and communalism.

Saleem's ideology suffers a revive jolt when he is relocated by his parents to Pakistan where he becomes isolated, still attuned to the stable India. Actually speaking, Saleem is autobiographical hero of Rushdie and Saleem's feeling of Pakistan is Rushdie's away, whether it is the Indo-Pak war of 1965 which brings disastrous end of his family (except Jamila) or anything else. He rushes back to India after Parvati's magic helps him. But India is not that of before; it is the emergency of 1975; he becomes to forget, is tortured to disclose the names and address of children of midnight who have to undergo irreversible utilization and other traumatic experience that finally brings profound change. Subsequently, the emergency is lifted but Saleem does not recover. The result is disillusionment and frustration and it is the account of the first 30 years of Independent India. Saleem gets his end and a new chapter begins in the history of India, created by Shiva. Aadam Sinai represents the generation of magical children born during emergency, more tough and resistant than the first one, more pragmatic spinner of a new myth, which is the need of the hour.

Saleem is exhausted now. Adam's mother Durga confirms it. This second generation is the synthesis of Shiva and Saleem whereas Saleem and Adam are synthesis of Indian colonials and contemporary India. Aadam is aware of his hybridity from the very beginning and does not bother for destiny and nation; Saleem is also the same; the result is the pessimistic ending of the novel; yet Saleem's painful guest for identity which is the chief characteristic of Indian Diasporic writing. Saleem is not in despair rather symbolizes the Indian talent of "non-stop self- regeneration" (1992:16). It hints at 'infinite possibilities' of the country and has optimistic flavor despite Saleem's personal tragedy.

It is said that the roaming triumph of *Midnight's Children* brought about a sort of renaissance in Indian writing in English for various reasons: its post-modern ingredients, historical interpretations, exuberant language, allegorical pattern, sexual overtones, and cinematic relevance, along with magical realism. Obviously the character of Saleem, Aadam, Aziz, Padma and Shiva—all represent the anxiety of Indian Diasporic writers to acquaint the readers with the contemporary India, its fragility and strength all inclusive.

Anita Desai and her characters are typical in the Indian Diasporic preview which can be detected in her work, for instance, in the novel *In Custody* which creates a world beyond the individual and not the internal consciousness. The protagonist of the novel is Deven Sharma, representing lower middle class family who is in search of self-fulfilment and so reaches out the outer wide world beyond his individual limitation. He is an average man with timid disposition and lethargic initiations and the plot of the novel centres around his weakness. For Deven, the responsibility of running a family in terms of marriage, job and earning livelihood is a meaningless exercise; he despises all these and finds himself trapped and caged; he seeks freedom and in his guest of liberty finds Urdu poet Nurshah Jehanabadi whom he interviews, records his memoirs, but all these end in a fiasco. There continuous failure forces him to see within, to introspect to find his inner strength.

Like other Diasporic novel, this novel does not go to shad east-west encounter or identity crisis, rather it is the conflict between the outer and inner world of an individual. The central character Deven is victim of circumstances or we can say that it is his failure to deal with his problems; he is a diffident and awkward hero with a background that may be called dreariness of Mirepare and Delhi. Deven is much more like Mirpore, dull and barren, desolate and airdate, mirthless and lifeless of dirt and dust has connotation of unproductivity, sterility and death which kills vitality, creativity and growth, prescisely, full of negative images. It was an uneventful life there where the violence of religious riots does not last long. Anita Desai calls it 'safe dustbin' for Deven. Moreover Deven's personal composition is hurdle in his development; he has a sense of insecurity inadequacy and habitual timidity; he is assailed by his own doubts and not others. The dullness, boredom and apathy of Mirpore is the essence of Deven too; even the promise and glory of Delhi cannot change him; he finds it "more crowded and chaotic" (33). Nur's Chandini Chowk does not fascinate him; he finds it decadent and degenerated. Nur's present inhabitant is a state of waste, neglect and lethargy- full of gloom and darkness. Deven's romantic vision of poets is stifled. Deven is equally trapped in Delhi and his fantasy is shattered. it is another facet of reality. This landscape also reflects the transition of society. By the end of the novel, Deven realizes the fact of life, the bitterness of reality and the importance of introspection. Deven is disillusioned of the outer materialistic world and search for alternatives; this disillusionment is a predominant characteristic of Indian Diasporic writing. Characters came to know the futility of unlimited yearning and venturing in the illusory world of fascinating exterior. All these finally lead to disenchantment and the need to read the internal world of an individual which may bring the knowledge of one's strength and weakness, for further improvement and betterment.

Anita Desai, undoubtedly, projects the inevitable conflicts and contradictions of life in quest of the authentic. As N.R. Shastri says:

> The quest is for the authentic able to experience plurality without giving up faith in the principle of creative ordering

> of this plurality into a significant pattern. Once a quest is seen as central, the narrative structures are more or less created to dramatize the resulting complex of motifs (159)

Deven's anxiety is futile because his Mirepore and Nur's Delhi share the common element of decay, decadence and disorder, as the rest of the world. Deven's reach for the ideal world is his utopian dream, never to be achieved; there is no reason for being 'small, weak and inadequate; his attempt to escape the stifling world of the small town succumbs to the nightmare of 'no exit' and it becomes recurrent throughout the novel. Deven fails to reconcile the order and harmony represented by Nur's Delhi; his journey to Delhi is a complicated yearning; he shuttles between Mirapore and Delhi which represents the period of transition. Deven persistent moral scrutiny is inherited, as well as paradoxical; it is a wave of romanticism and nothing else; Desai calls it "Mortal myopia and stupidity" (39) and Deven considers it 'epiphany movement of sheer ecstasy'. Deven's tendency is to imbue the part with a truth of meaning and significance which can be sustained at the level of fantasy. The memory of his father is refracted through fantasy, the tool of the narrative which cannot change the part but romanticize it; the way his father apologizes before his mother for the little he could do in the part influences Deven, in his turn as father; this is the juxtaposition of the ideal and the real. Nur is altogether different as a poet-greedy, senile, lustful man and surrounded by sycophants. Nur constantly makes claim on Deven for money and delicacies. Deven's life at Mirapore is life of "non-events, non-happenings-empty and hopeless; safe-and endurable"(184). Deven had imagined Nur to be ascetic and magical genius, instead he found him weak and grasping whose days of creativity had came to an end. He finds a technique to distinguish between his art and personality, the creature and the sufferer, the artist and the man. Nur at times appear to be enigmatic as an unanswerable question and contrary to the ideal frame of Deveen. It is here that Deven can realize that art is also influenced by political and economic factors of human existence. It is a bitter truth that literary excellence is dependent on political patronage. As N.R. Shastri concludes:

> *In Custody*... reflects Anita Desai's usual preoccupations: the guest for authenticity flowed from the beginning by force of history, further distasted by fantasies, bypassing the past. (168)

And Deven remains an anxious adventure in search of true definition of art and its manifestations: the changing face of art, its diverse effects, its mysterious nature both a communication and an escape, an instrument of power and an unanswerable question. His final decision to flee to states is discouraged by the prospect for the languages and humanities. There is no future before him so he goes back to the past, for him Nur is art who can offer no explanation and no solution to any problems. His final moving out of the house without telling his wife, walking aimlessly reveals his utter frustration and the final disenchantment, and this is typical of a Diasporic character: search for ideal, caught in dilemma and ultimate realization.

Pessimism and despair also haunts the world of Indian Diasporic writings and their characters are inevitably victim to such depressing and disastrous circumstances. Another important writer under discussion is Rohintar Mistry who happens to be settled in Canada, but actually is an Indian Parsi writer. Let us take his novel A Fine Balance, winner of the prestigious commonwealth writers prize in 1996. The opening of the novel is remarkable for the Balzac quote "this tragedy is not a fiction. All is true."

As we know, the constitution of a novel comprises plot, theme, language and character, and, of course, the place, that is, the location. Essentially a novel is bound up in the local, the real, the present and the day-to-day experience of life—and this novel is all about India, a literary voyage, an attempt to revision the history of his homeland, his community and family—all these explained with the help of Diasporic consciousness through characters who undergo the jolting experience.

The post-Independent India has witnessed several crises which affected the common people of India through socio-political-cultural turmoil. History, undeniably, affects the personal lives of common people be it Dina Dalal, Ishvar Darji, Omprakash or Maneek Kohlahi. Mistry has to move to the middle class of both rural and urban population, and the educating mass. The age-old disease of the country is brought forward, for instance, the atrocities committed on the untouchables, the dominance of Zamindars (the Thakurs), the exploitation and injustice of the colonizers, and, of course, the caste system and gender discrimination. The atmosphere of the after Independent India is also not so sweet and satisfactory, because in the name of democracy, new political leaders are playing game of conspiracy and atrocities with their corrupt and maligned attitude. Obviously the condition is unchanged: first it was the era of Zamindars, then came the colonizers and Independence brought the political leaders in the name of democracy – all are same with same attitude but different nomenclature; the time of Mrs. Gandhi and her emergency is not to be forgotten. Buddha as the name goes is not a full really but victim of the caste system and Zamindari system and so is Dukhi. Then comes the story of Ishvar and Omprakash whose grievances are that of a migratory bird; in the new home of Bombay they are again downtrodden the slum dwellers and they have the anguish, pain, anxiety and restlessness of people away from their native place—so the question of belongingness, of identity crisis, of the sense of deprivation, of the sense of being marginal—all came together for them.

The novel also discuss another complexity of Indian society, that is, gender discrimination, and the victim is Dina, though she symbolizes the 'new women' because she refuses to be submissive and marries Rustam Dalal. Diva does not accept the stereotypical feminine role and even after the death of her first husband resolves to restructure her life instead of wailing a being dependant on a man, economically or otherwise. Dina is the strongest character of the novel: progressive and independent. Mistry also highlights the evils of the Indian camp where Maneek and Avinash who go for nepotism, bribery, ragging, preferences to political elites, corruption in sale of examination forms, etc; the interference of the politicians, the east, intimidation of faculty members and student politics in campus is also discussed.

The mysterious death of Avinash adds a new chapter in the prevailing nasty world. Mistry also gives due weightage to communal riots between Hindu and Muslims and Sikh riots of 1984.

In fact, *A Fine Balance* is a true and realistic picture of the post-Independent India presented by a Canada settled Indian writer and the characters here are true and real as envisioned by a Diasporic writer who finally aggress to the intimate relationship among the fair characters: Dina, Om, Maneek and Ishvar, by making a fine balance between success and failure hope and despair, and change and adoption—this is also the secret of the lives of immigrants. The most interesting character is that of Maneek Kahlal who suffers double displacement are is geographical and the other is emotional which is not less important. It was the time of Emergency and its ill effects could be seen all around; Maneek is also a victim of the repressive political atmosphere, though later on he realizes his escapist nature and his escapist tendencies and finally decides to go for suicide. Emotional upheavals and anchors mar Dina's progression of life; she also has acute sense of displacement, more emotional than physical. There is dichotomy in her life, the result of her short-lived marriage with Rustam Dalal, her affairs with Freedom, her brief tailoring enterprises, her brothers ill behaviors, the land lards physical assault- and taken together it farms a cyclic life. Precisely, all characters reveal Diasporic consciousness of belongingness and identity crisis.

Belongingness is the chief concern in Indian diaspara writing and its characters are always caught between two cultures, languages and space which results in anxious sense of dislocation, the question of homelessness and the haunting nostalgia. This dilemma of displacement can be traced in almost all writings and characters. Here we take the works of Bharati Mukherjee. Her characters are mostly from the lot of Indians living abroad. The writing is different from others because it is very much related with her personal life and some critics call it a 'political act'. As a woman, she has a very strong sense of marginalization and racial discrimination including colour.

Days and Nights in Calcutta (1977) tells her paradoxical position and the two novels *The Tiger's Daughter* (1971) and *Wife* (1975) record her personal trauma. Tara and Dimple are the protagonists of the two novels who are doubly displaced: geographically and emotionally. Like any expatriate, they are not at ease in the native and alien cultures and suffer from solitude and alienation. Assimilation is almost impossible, and if at all it happens, it is partial and does not involve the denial of the part; so they like in a dual world, in a state of 'fluid identity'. Darkness is a collection of stories which have many things to convey.

Ratna, an Indian lady married to Canadian professor Graeme Clayton are out on a holiday at an island off the coast of Africa to see the Southern Cross to convince Ratna to shift to Toronto from Montreal. She has fear and insecurity of leaving her old habitat but her husband is indifferent to her choice. He has accepted the chair of personality Development at Toronto so Ratna does not matter to him. Ratra's identity is at stake and her expatriate existence makes difference in her ignorance.

In the story 'Isolated Incidents' the common attitude of a common Canadian towards an expatriate is presented. The instance here is that of Ann Vane who is reluctant to record the cares of John Mohan Persawd and Miss Supariwalla for the simple reason that they were racially different.

In the story Hindus' Bharati Mukharjee juxtaposes an expatriate against an immigrant and brings out the contrast through the narrator of the story Leda Lahri. Once again, the concept of 'fluid identity' is vivid though she claims that she is Bengali Brahmin and American. H.R.H. Maharajah Patwant Singh of Gotlah is an expatriate having grievances against it, after two years he is found to be writing memories, of woes. Leela enjoys her new identity as an immigrant yet she does not deny her part and admits her dual existence. Their stories are fragmented and the characters in a world of nostalgia starve for a home, identity and status; assimilation is the main question and belongingness is the main anxiety; they are tarn between the old and new world and suffer from inferiority complex. The stories are open-ended and inconclusive, an authoritative interpretation of crucial moments of expatriate life, and an acknowledgement of alternative realities; in a positive wag it provides opportunity to acquaint us with two cultures and redefine over hopes, aspirations and destination, for culture is an even changing process and not a static dead fabric.

Let us take the case of Kiran Desai, the daughter of Anita Desai who could gather the prestigious Man Booker prize of 2006 for her book *The Inheritance of Loss* which is basically a Diasparic articulation, and when we talk of Diaspora, inevitably certain questions prop up, that is, of cultural confrontation, identity crisis, belongingness and home. The bitter experience of any immigrant is related to all these aspects but with the changing human relations, impact of globalization and post-colonial chaos the problem has become more and more complicated. With Kiran's Diasporic experience, she could create characters of different sorts who can be categorized, primarily, into two types one who have not tasted the alien dish and the other who are caught between the native and the alien. The character of the Indians who have never been abroad is not so important in this prospective but the character of the second type is important for our present study and in this category falls Biju, Saeed, Harish, Harry, Saran, Jeev, Rishi, and Mr. Lalkaka; there are thousands of Africans, Latin Americans and Asians working in America and Europe, with the same kind of bitter experience of immigrants. Biju moves from one pillar to another without a green card but cannot find a good job and it continues for 30 years; he is one of those who lived and died illegal in America. Same is the lot of Saeed, he also has the same authentic colonial experience, racial discrimination being one of them. While studying in England Jemu also faces all these problems. Finally they are disillusioned by the West.

When a character is torn between two cultures, the maximum possibility is that of loss of culture and this loss of culture brings about loss of identity and loss of human relations—then things have been discussed at length in Kiran Desai's *The Inheritance of Loss*. Taken together it brings about a huge loss, call it, loss of emotional binding, human values, rationality, faith, peace, harmony, etc. and it becomes integral part of every character's life, a way of life. There are negative developments and make the characters insecure, unmoved and isolated, left alone to struggle to survive in the modern world. In the alien world their Indian heritage brings them discomfort and uncase and they become scapegoat of so many things. Jemu is character who goes to Cambridge for higher studies selected in I.C.S., and becomes a judge but the Western values chase him, he cannot abandon them, consequently, he loses his Indian identity and becomes ridiculous. It is their Anglophilia that brings self-hatred for them and they become unwanted anachronism of the society which is no more ignorant, rather awakened to their dereliction in their emotional outburst of anger and despair.

Desai cites the instance of GNLF movement and Gyan's xenophobia and Jemu's neurosis. Jemu has atypical character of split personality, a divided soul and a disintegrated soul: he envies the English and despises the Indians. The arrival of Biju, sai and GNLF activities disturbs his life and strongly misses the glorious part.

Desai talks of the North East and discusses its restlessness, the problem of emergency, the loss of culture and the three loses, "Tea, Timber, Tourism" (225). Another character Sai also loses indigenous cultural values in the process of academic learning in a convent school where the Western Christian values are imbibed and the result is division in her personality, "full of contradictions"(30). Identity crisis is her another character and her profound loss is that of the loss of Gyan Biju's dream and hope are shattered in New York and he can experience authentic colonial experience, the exploitation and humiliation of the Third World poor natives in the west. Kiran Desai writes:

> They drew the lines at crucial junctures—On the top, rich colonial, and down below, poor native; Columbian, Tunisian, Ecuadorian—above all, the restaurant was French but below In the kitchen it was Mexican and Indian—There was a whole world in the basement kitchens of New York (21-23)

The Indians were addressed as "Uloo ka patta, son of an owl, low down son-of-a-bitch Indian" (22). The characters have to face discrimination at every step: in the laws of immigration, in procuring green cards; as a result Biju's character evolve as a geneses figure, representing young men, easily termed as 'crazy men of the Third World', bound to face tough onwards in the alien land. similarly, other characters like Lola, Nani, Pixie and Mrs. Sen are also victims of British regulations; almost all characters of Desai find themselves trapped and are stunted by their encounters with the alien culture, civilization and regulations.

Kamala Mankandaya is another diasporic writer with adequate understanding of both the east and the West, as Bhatnagar points out:

> She is an impressive explorer of human consciousness and of the convulsions of intimate interpersonal relationship caught in the whirlpool of disparate and divergent cultures. (2)

Let us take the instance of her novel *Pleasure City*. It is the confluence of Orient and Occident; Rikki representing the Orient and Tully presenting the occident and their friendship is the meeting pointing of the two cultures and dissolution of two identities. Tully is an English officer and imbibes transcontinental consortium with the touch of modern technology who has came to the South India for fishing and seeks to transform the Village by building 'Shalimar', a holiday complex a French area of understanding and cooperation to bring together the two cultures, for development and prosperity. Kamala Markandaya calls the entrance of imperialist in the disguise of technocrats, modernity and progress. Rikki has a different perception of beauty and honesty, and a sense of spiritualism, inherited from the Indian culture. Rikki tries to bring a synthesis between the two cultures, and the Village is the witness to this novel Endeavour. Rikki is a common land who goes for schooling in the ordinary school of fisherman. He loses his father when he was only six years old and subsequently his mother also; Amma, the wife of the headman Apu becomes her foster mother and takes care of him along with her own children Muthu and Valli. He gets the love and affection of Mr and Mrs Briddie, the owner of the school who also meet their death. In her landlines and dejection she meets Tully in Shalimar, a storm bursts out and Corrina is caught in the wild storm; Rikki goes to save her and is badly hurt. The Atlas International Development Corporation take initiative to help the victims of the storm and Tully takes care of Rikki personally, it is the story of love and affection, feeling and understanding, and friendship and meeting, that opens a new chapter of possibilities of dissolution of dichotomy between the native and the alien, on the foundation of Rikki-Tully friendship which is a sort of 'Assimilation', which Bhatnagar points out, as:

> friendship of moderns and traditionals—points to fresh areas of understanding and cooperation between the east and the west in the post colonial period.—this is how the two parts of World can contribute their migh of the development and prosperity Of each other—Tully is a decolonized Prospero returning to expiate the Crimes of the part, searching for a spiritual home and place. The Spiritual journey undertaken by Tully in the company of Rikki, is a regressive journey from civilization, but a journey of progression towards complete decolonization. (49-111)

Rikki believes in human relationship and is basically unselfish, that is why he tells his sister Valli that Tully is "human as you or me" (73). "Despite the friendship between Rikki and Tully' there is an ocean of difference between the two and Rikki feels it at most:

> between one man and other, their minds, Their reach and sway, the reality Of the distance between himself and Tully. Distance? Notes of incredulity sounded as well. Distance between them, chipping at marble in the pool room together shaving the light, and emotions? Where was the reality, what was vapour? Presently he had to lay down the chisel and simply sit, wondering, looking full face at Tully. (147)

So the friendship becomes a myth. But Tully demytholises it, "For was there an ocean? Actually? His incredulity echoes

Rikki's". But Kamala Markandaya cannot isolate the Rikkis, and manipulates to wash away the shadow lines of demarcation of the landscape "washed over them like water or light, and merged them into the one landscape" (147). Finally the test of 'pleasure city' becomes the Bible of assimilation of the two cultures:

> A two-way deal, getting to know one's fellow, advancing beyond language to contemplation, contemplating another human, most complex of beings, each engaged in a voyage of discovery no less strenuous, or ravishing, than a physical adventure. (81)

Obviously, Kamala Markandaya's protagonist does not suffer from any complicacy (neither Tully nor Rikki) as any other Diasporic writing because of the congenial climate created by his; certainly this is an exception.

The East-West encounter is an important theme of Indian Diasporic writing, and Nargis Dalal comes under the same bracket. We can take the instance of her novel *The Girls from Overseas*. Larise, Michalle, Sandy, Jane and Gertrude—all these girl characters are stationed in Dehra Dun; they meet at one or other of their houses once a week, for coffee, talk of their husbands, children, in-laws and other problems which they encounter, so we can call the meeting as confessional' or 'safety valve analysts'. Michelle, the French woman, is married to General Raj who is untouched by the Indian influence, though she has spent more than 40 years in India; she has been able to retain her identity. Another pair is that of Jane and Sunil spending an unhappy conjugal life. Jane has a strong sense of hatred for Indians like her mother, which is why she despises her mother-in- law and sister-in-law; none of them are accommodative, and Jane is taken as an outsider. She has an illicit relationship with Jason and the marriage with Sunil is a fake assertion of togetherness. In the same novel we have another pair Louise and Dinesh which is, again, a sick conjugal life. Louise is a Canadian married to Dinesh, an engineer. The reason for dissatisfaction is the mother-in-law in particular and other family members in general. The resentment spreads to the whole country of India. Her love for Dinesh is matchless;

she likes her daughter Sonia also but India does not suit her. The novel has yet another pair that of Sandy and Dilip, where Dilip is, probably, important and the marriage remains a mistake, somehow incorrigible. Dilip is a rich jeweller and Sandy an outspoken extrovert American, they have everything except a successful sexual life. Another unhappy couple is that of Gertrude and George Das: Das is a boozer and womanizer but ignores his wife vehemently, and the marriage becomes a disaster and the death of their sick child aggravates the tragedy. Gertrude fails to identify with the country, *strikes* to her identity and retains her 'separateness'. All the couples in the novel are dissatisfied for the same reason, but the main reason is that all the female characters belong to the alien land and they are unable to cope with the existing culture. The problem is that of compromise, that of assimilations, and that of understanding.

As we know, the Diaspora communities are bound to live in multicultural environments and the obvious result is a sort of re-identification and reassignment to the self for the struggle for survival and existence, which can be termed as reassembly of the self, or say, reconstructing of the self to face the new alien world as the 'other', by relocating the self in the third space of multiculturalism. Here identity becomes important as an individual for the sole purpose of self and in respect of society. *The Middleman and Other Stories* of Bharati Mukharjee and *Arranged Marriage* of Chitra Banarji Devikaruni may be cited to highlight the reconstruction of the individual and self particularly in the case of woman in an alien, in loneliness. For the inhabitants of the East, the West is a dreamland, a land of fairy tales where all aspirations can be fulfilled; for Indian women a "handsome prince who took her to his kingdom beyond the seven seas; (*Arranged*,18); for Jayanti in 'Silver pavements', it is a 'no problem' Zone, 'land of Almond Rocas'. Jayanti is thrilled on her journey to the new land and feels pity for her friends in the native land. She suffers the problem of non-identity in her native land where women are taken least care in the patriarchal society. She longs for the American dream, financial stability and the end of 'otherness' Western concept of liberty, democracy and freedom attracts them. But the fact is different, in the Diasporic world; the Indian community has to face a new world of multiculturalism where identity is always under threat, social and racial discrimination is always torturing and this section of society is labelled as 'nigger' a derogatory term. Jayanti has to face all these problems; she has to face her aunt to take a stroll in the neighbourhood country to her wishes; they are attacked by a group of pre-teenage boys. In fact, in America, Indians are grouped together with Africans and treated as slaves. Patriarchy is there also in the West, rather women find themselves trapped in more burden, that of, maintaining kinship network, religious and cultural traditional norms. So they have to carve their own niche, give up the previous identity and Jayanti says, "can't they see that I'm not black at all but an Indian girl of good family"(51). All the time, the dichotomy of life is perplexing, "Should I wear the colourful Indian clothes that I love, or should I quit wearing them in public because I am tired of being stared at? Should I keep my hard-to-pronounce Hindu name, or should I Anglicize it like many Chinese had done? Should I celebrate Christmas, a tradition that I didn't grow up with or ... celebrate Diwali, the most important Indian holiday."

Such dilemmas are suffocating to the Diasporic communities. These writers observe everything very minutely. They feel that even clothes are a kind of statement, rather important statement, a metaphorical representation of the stages of hope, despair and reconciliation. The most astonishing character is that of Sumita, brought up in a traditional Indian family structure with the ingrained belief that a married woman belongs to her husband and her in-laws only, she should not visit any public place, and so many restriction like that; and the crux of the matter lies in unquestioning acceptance of all these norms, like a dead wood, like a lifeless object. Somesh is her husband and tries his best to satisfy her dream with whatever is available in California; California has everything, there is no question of any kind of dearth or scarcity and it reveals her financial stability. She is linked to the past with the gift of the mother and now comes the question of jeans and shirts—the question of double existence; she has imbibed the Western values. With her widowhood everything is changed and she finds herself "inside this glass world, watching helplessly as America rushes by, wanting to scream" (26). She is aware of the options before her and she rejects the idea of going back to India where widows are imprisoned and wishes to remain in America. India is anachronistic to immigrant writers and they recreate artificial India in the alien land, with mock marriages and likewise. This is both fictional and factional account of India unaware of the recent changes that India has undergone, both social and attitudinal.

Another character Sheila is of the same attitude when she decides to reject her past for the sake of a better future in 'The Management of Grief. She is Bharati Mukherjee's widow who is unable to conform to the tradition in which her grandmother had done as harbinger of bad luck; such as getting the head shaved, living in separate quarters and cooking with servants her own food; her parents are progressive and do not agree with such mindless mortification; however the widows have not to suffer that wag. The alien culture does not allow anything like that.

There is another widow 'Kusum' who takes refuge in the spiritualism of India but her adopted daughter defies the mother's choice and goes for the West, different from her sisters, "My sister is an expatriate, professionally generous and creative, socially courteous and gracious, and that's as far as her Americanization can go." Kusum resolves the crisis by ending her exile and going back to India and her immigrant daughter survives all her connections with it.

Kusum and Sheila are the two widows with two different mental set up. Sheila tries to make the India culture futile and does not look for any answer in it; in an abandoned temple in the Himalayas she feels the preserve of her husband, it may be her alter-ego, and then comes the incident of encounter with a fake *sadhu* who tries to molest her and it puts an end to India for ever. So these characters are torn between the two differences. No doubt, an expatriate woman character has multiple options in the multicultural world which is divorced from the roles of 'passivity' acceptance and subservience, yet there are boundaries of immigrant selves; the choices are limited.

The setting, the character and the point of view—they go in the constitution of a novel. A reader moves with characters in the landscape of the novel, in the milieu of the times: the social, political, economic and religious conditions of the local—and all these go in the shaping of the characters. Precisely, the characters of Diaspora writing are never sound and integrated; all of them suffer from the compulsions of the West; the clash of culture bring about annoying dimension to their personality; they alter their present; their whole life is that of compromise and negotiations; and all the time, the question of belongingness, homelessness, loneliness and identity troubles him. In this wag, all these characters are not fictions, rather characters coming out of the lives of the Diasporic writers themselves.

Works Cited

Bhatnagar, M.K., (ed.), *Kamala Markandya : A Critical Spectrum,* New Delhi : Atlantic, 2002.

Joshi, N.R., Narrative Strategy Of Anita Desai's *In Custody. Critical Responses: Commonwealth Literature,* Deptt. Of English, Osmania University Hyderabad, Sterling Pub. New Delhi, 1993..

Markandya, Kamala, *Pleasure City*, London : Chatto & Windus, 1982.

Mehta, Gita, *Snakes and Ladders: A View of Modern India,* London: Minerva Paperbacks, 1997.

Rushdie, Salman, *Midnight's Children*, London: Pan Books, 1983.

———*Imaginary Homelands: Essays on Criticism 1981-91*, London: Granta, 1992.

Said, Edward, *Culture and Imperialism,* London: Vintage, 1993.

4

Plan Behind the Set-up

Indian Diaspora writers move with a certain plan in their mind to present before the world the factual status of the Diasporic world, for the simple reason that readers are annoyed with imaginary fictious world, and creative writing is a legitimate record of the ongoings of an individual and his society; to have a close view of such plans, we will have to examine certain texts, their layouts and their contents.

Let us take the women writers first. In *The Indian Writer's Problems*, Anita Desai admits:

> By writing novels that have been catalogued by critics as psychological and that are purely subjective, I have been left free to employ, simply language of the interior. Even when two characters meet, they use this particular type of language—the language of their thoughts, their interior selves—which has nothing to do with geography and can be written in any language. (225)

Obviously, the plan behind Anita Desai's writing is to expose the interior self, its feeling, its experience and its responses; here, political and social realities relegate to the back seat; consequently, her characters become introvert, speak less and react more, and find themselves trapped. We can examine her work *Fire on the Mountain* which fetched her the most coveted award of Sahitya Akademi in 1978. The most striking idea, central to the novel, is the question of the protagonist Nanda Kaul, "Can I not be left with nothing?" Her present life is that of recluse and she wants to delink herself from the life of her past, the part which was the best of her life; but complete divorce from the past is not possible. The winter creates a climate of the upper class society with Nanda Kaul who happens to be the wife of the Vice Chancellor, tasted the bitter sweetness of the sophisticated manners and now she is fed up with all that.

Anita Desai creates Carignano, the place of her preference and dream, and, "She wanted no one and nothing else. Whatever else came, or happened here, would be an unwelcome distractions" (3). So it is not loneliness alone, ratter it is loneliness created, invited and nourished. Desai has a beautiful landscape in her mind and so is her Carignano. It is Desai's utopia, a land of freedom, "To be a free, no more and no less was all, she was prepared to undertake" (4). It is a world of complete withdrawal, of emotional stativity, of psychic frigidity and complete stillness.

Her peaceful world is shattered by her daughter's letter, but she again goes to the book *The Pillow Book of Scishonagon* and opens the chapter 'A Women Lives Alone'—so it is again the drive for loneliness; there is no place for an intruder or outsider. With Raka, the writer wants to disturb the stillness of Nanda Kaul's world of 'not exist'. The funniest thing is that both Nanda Kaul and Raka prefer seclusion, one out of vengeance and the other out of nature, but they can feel the annoying presence of the other. By and by, the silence is broken, communication between the two commences, Nanda shares her experience; her firm 'no' is dissolved and the desire of loneliness is gone, and she feels, 'you are more like me—exactly like me'. Raka tries to enter the mainstream but soon disillusioned. Now Raka can understand the significance of Carignano but Nanda is a bit perplexed. Nanda gets the news of Raka's mother's breakdown but does not communicate it to her, instead, she engages her in fabricated stories. The role of Ila Das is not substantial in the novel and her murder is also mysterious.

Anita Desai has carved out a pattern that cannot be falsified. She has painted the top class consciousness and the aristocratic temperament of the educated top ranking Indians, the class consciousness, Nanda's option for loneliness and Ila Das, recall of her past. This is a woman's world: Nanda Kaul,

Raka and Ila. Ila represents the fate of poor educated women turned into a social worker; Nanda Kaul represents the destiny of a dissatisfied wife of a man of high rank, like a forest fire, ever burning, like a dream dreamt by others; and Raka represents an unwanted disturbing soul which fails a novel attempt of Nanda's wish of solitude. It may be interpreted otherwise: Ila representing attachment to self, Nanda representing detachment and Raka representing the indifference.

This is a world which poses threat to woman's safety, their happiness and their ulterior wish to live a life of their own; so it is a world of dilemma, of confusion, of agency, of anxiety—all for women only.

Anita Desai's execution of plan is exquisite. Jasbir Jain is of the view:

> Desai uses fantasyy not only for creating an alternative reality but also for contrasting the two or more visions of reality projected in particular work of fiction (1992:227).

Her *Bye-Bye Blackbird* (1985) ceases to be a native world, rather it is a typical world of migration with a dream and the subsequent disillusionment and is between the thread of vanity, identity, nostalgia and exploitation. It is a well-planned world, well pursued and well established to exhibit her wonderland of futility.

Dev moves to London to pursue his studies, fails to acclamatize, feels alienated, encounters cultural shocks becomes self-conscious, feels humiliated and unwanted, and so and so forth, as her divulges to Adit, his London-settled friend:

> You would sell your soul and your passport too, for a glimpse at two shillings, of some draughty old stately home. (19)

The Indian culture comes to his memory; the feeling of friendliness, call it the world of fellow feeling or love and affection, and he says:

> If this were India—I would by now know all my neighbors-even if I had spoken to them. I'd know their taste ... study ... exam. (56)

The life at London is silent and invisible, strong and hidden, empty and tasteless, lifeless and dead:

> The English habit of keeping all doors and windows tightly shut...of guarding their throats from catching cold, cannot quite be explained to him by the facts of the cold and the rain. (63)

Dev has developed a sense of hatred for everything which London possesses, even the churches and hesitates to enter London School of Economics:

> There are days in which the life of an alien appears enthrallingly rich and beautiful to him, and that of a homebody too dull, too stale to return to ever. Then he hears a word in the tube or notices an expression on an English face that overturns his latest decision and drawing himself together, he feels he can never bear to be the unwanted immigrant but must return to his own land, however, object or dull, where he has, at least, a place in the sun, security, status and freedom (86).

Obviously, it is a question of identity and belongingness for which any individual can long for, and particularly a man of Indian origin and Indian culture. Dev finds London all uncomfortable where he won't be able to translate his dreams:

> He was slowly regretfully letting drop and melt away his dreams of adventure, seeing now quite clearly that he had left the true land of adventure of the unexpected, the spontaneous, the wild and the weird, for a very enclosed part of the world, a pigeoncote in which it was necessary to find an empty and warm niche before one was pushed over the ledge into the sea that lapped the island's stony shores. (104)

If Dev has to be successful in London he must be a Christian, a Catholic and not an Indian or a Hindu, if so he won't get a job; so the parameter is different:

> Not a Catholic? Not even Christian? I am sorry, Dear me, I ought to have mentioned it at once—we simply must have a Catholic, or at least a High Church man. It's public relations... . I'm afraid it wouldn't do to have a Hindu gentleman in this job. (108)

He wonders whether he had opted for becoming another 'Macaulay's bastard' and so he thinks:

> ...how it was that so many people in his country, of so many generations and so many social and economic classes had been brought up on a language and literature completely alien to them (122)

He feels that he is wasting his time there, not engrossed in the studies of politics, philosophy and economics, rather he is:

> ...an ambassador. I am showing these damn imperialists with their lost colonies complex that we are free people now, with our personalities, that this vaneer of English education has not obscured and not afraid to match ours with theirs, I am here—to interpret my country to them, to conquer England as they once conquered India. (123)

He finds himself entangled, trapped and suffocated. He has "to seek, to discover and win the England of his dreams ... the most poetic—the most innocent and enduring" (168).

Adit is completely contrary to Dev. Despite the problem of identity crisis, Anita Desai projects him as a romantic admirer of England; he doesn't find any drawbacks in the English system; he has a negative impression of India:

> I only notice the laziness of the clerks and the unpunctuality of the buses and trains and the beggars and the flies and the stench- and the boredom—then I am mad to go back to England. (49)

He is content with the "nice warm pubs—glass of Guinness and the girls" (49). He is not in doubt or dilemma; he believes in the present and doesn't think more, and is not worried at all. In that way, Adit has been projected as a pragmatic fellow, as he says:

> I never called myself a prophet or a saint. I only said I would occupy India House with same style, dining on the riches *murgh mussallam* and *chicken biryani,* serving liquors from Jaipur brewed of pigeons blood and pearls and dazzling everyone with my oriental wit and fluency. (154)

Yet, the 'emptiness and melancholy' of India, Bismillah Khan's *Shehnai*, sweet mango *chutney*, the landscapes—all that has become a past calls him back to India and thus grows nostalgia within him. It may appear incomprehensible altitude; on the one hand, the placidity, the munificence and the case of the alien land and on the other, its slights and insults. While talking to Sarah he says:

> ... you'll never accept anything but your own drab, dingy standards and your own dull, boring ways. Anything else looks clownish to you, laughable. (193)

He oscillates between the two worlds of his native land and the attractions of the alien soil and so he says to Sarah:

> I tell you. I've had enough. It's all got to end now. There must be a change. A- a big change. I've got to do it. You- you understand? Now don't stop me, don't say anything. I've made up my mind. No- England. I've done worth England now. Sarah, I'm going back.
>
> It has no reality at all, we just pretend all the time. I'm twenty seven now. I've got to go home and start living a real life. I don't know what real life there will mean." (203-4)

Anita Desai projects Adit as a torn character, divided between the East and the West. Earlier he had declared that he was half-English but now he admits that it was a pentence only; Sarah as a loyal wife is ready to give birth to her new baby in India; and Adit feels:

> an exile with memories of the reality that had been refreshed now that he was forced to be realistic, and with his growing worries of the changes that had taken place at home since he left. (213)

The turmoils of England made to choose between the life at London and that of India, between the country home in Hampshire and overpopulated Calcutta, between his wife's kitchen at London and that of his mother, untidy and unclean. Now he begins to believe that Indians are inferior in every way; yet he was connected to that land because of his wife Sarah.

On the other hand, Sarah loves India, its lifestyle and its values, though she suffers from identity crisis. She does not like English people's love for privacy and reserve; like Adit she is also hung between two cultures, and she feels:

> ... to discuss her Indian husband, would have forced her to parade like an impostor, to make claims to a life, an identity, that she did not herself feel to be her own. (37)

But the fake swamis, yogic postures and the ills like those disenchanted her gradually,

> There was the baby. There was the voyage- the uprooting. And all at a time when she felt capable of doing no more than quietly sitting down and quietly cradling her child inside the fluids that rocked and heaved inside her body. (206)

Sarah knows the difference, the things of which her child would be deprived of:

> She began rapidly to draw up list of things her child would not know and enjoy and tried to stop herself by attending to another list of things the child would know and enjoy, but in spite of the substantial length of this list, she could help biting her lip's and casting another look at the pleasures it would have to forego. (223)

Anita Desai in her novel *Bye Bye Blackbird,* projects the characters who suffer from identity crisis, self-alienation and subsequent disenchantment. This is a planned move of the author to highlight the ingredients of two cultures, the positive and negative aspects of two societies which compel the characters to undergo self-analysis and the elements of reality. It is a real world of Diasporic individuals, which is bound to be divided and torn. On the one hand, there is a dream of a prosperous world in the West, and on the other, there is a pull of the love and benevolence of the native land; the Diasporic identity has to settle between the two. This is the world of dilemma, a riddle that can never be solved.

Frankly speaking, we have to indicate the fact that a creative writer acts as a planner and diasoric writers move with the same target in their mind to expose the world in a planned way with the help of plot, characters and climate. Rohinto Mistry falls in the same line who speaks for Parsi Diasporas, their identity, their territory and their belongingness; he talks of Parsi identity and in territory he talks of cultural territory, for the simple reason, that the Parsis are a dilapidated community, a depraved community with a glorious past and perilous present. His first novel *Such a Long Journey* not only problematizes the Parsi Diaspora in the Indian context but also projects his anti-colonial resistance; all characters of this fiction are chosen from the middle class Parsi background resisting the snares of power in their own characteristic way; in the process the struggle between power and resistance go on.

Mistry plans to reveal the dynamics of power structures within hierarchies by displaying three categories and by establishing hegemonies through modes of resistance exhibited by different characters in confrontation with contention of power. Gustad Noble is the protagonist whose life in nothing but a large rhythm of patterns of empowerment with modes of resistance. His grandfather was a prosperous furniture dealer with a love for tasteful living and hence those were the days of heyday for his family. In his childhood Gustad enjoyed the luxuries of his grandfather's lavish lifestyle and his father's love for looks and his book store; all these things come to an end with his uncle who happened to be an alcoholic and a gambler. His father's parental loyalty can not rescue his share of parental property and this is the initiation of resistance of patriarchal authority, losing all sources of income. Now Gustard is financially and socially pitiable, living in a two-room flat in Khodadad Building with his wife, two sons and a daughter. He is a bank clerk with his meagre income with nostalgia and dream to regain his lost prosperity through Shorab, his eldest son who gets through IIT but refuses to join.

For the first time, in Diaspora writing, we find resistance to the parental authority, and that too, without substantial reason; it is a personal betrayal, probably another pattern of empowerment. Like other Diaspora novels *Such a Long Journey* doesn't dwell on the common Diasporic problems; as a Diasporic community Parsis' fate in India is under security; and so the hurdle of political power and corruption come in the way as a pattern of empowerment and the character made responsible is Major Jimmy trapped by the snares of political power and corruption; arrested on the charge of extorting Rs. 60 lakh from the bank by impersonating Prime Minister's voice. Jimmy appears to be fictional counterpart of Sohrab who was arrested and exterminated during Indira Gandhi's regime, an incident which had jolted the whole Parsi community, their image and their entity. This is Mistry's exclusive technique to re-enact his persona to vindicate the repugnance of his community as well as every politically conscious citizen of the world community; this is a vehement resistance as he says:

> ...assuring that Mr. Bilimoria has the talent of voice impersonation, is it routine for our National Banks to hand over the vast sums of man if the Prime Minister telephones? How high up does one have to be in the Govt. or the Congress Party to be able to make such a call? And was the chief cashier so familiar with Mrs. Gandhi's voice that he accepted the instructions without any verification whatsoever? If yes, does that mean that Mrs. Gandhi has done this sort of thing frequently. (195)

Mistry also attacks superpowers like USA for their international domination, the inhuman killing unleashed on Bangladesh by Pakistan Army with a tacit financial and armament support of America to block Russia's access to Indian ocean, etc. Such criticisms tinged with erotic metaphor not only intensify Mistry's discourse, they also focus the post-colonial resistance to the neo-colonizer USA.

In fact, this novel is an account of the post- Independence dilemma of the minorities like Parsi community. Before Independence they had enjoyed the privileges of power and social status by owing allegiance to the colonial masters, now they are forced to the periphery both socially and politically, and this is remarkable for any reader who wishes to know the progression of society. In the present scenario of the emergence of fundamentalism and linguistic movement as the yardstick for determining national allegiance sidelined the 'religious other', the Muslims, and the 'cultural other'—the Parsis, etc.—Mistry's concern is voiced by Gustad evocatively and frankly:

> No future for minorities with the fascist Shivsena politics and Marathi language nonsense. It was to be like the black people in America as good as Whiteman to get half as much. (76)

So it is the question of identity, a question of belongingness, a question of existence. Mistry is similar to the other post-colonial writers in his posing challenge to the elite masters and privileging the marginals as resistance to the Western hegemony. As a Parsi, he is Diaspora to the Indian soil and finds himself marginalized and at periphery, so this Diasporic fiction should be taken as resistance to the tantalization of dominant culture within India itself, and thus problematises the Diasporic dilemma; it also questions the post-colonial writings for its paradigms and reins vibe normative texts; this is the second stage of anticolonial resistance against the socio-cultural domination of the colonizer the British and the neo-colonizer that is USA, known as cultural nationalist phase—a fight for distinct identity.

A less known warm writer is Shantha Rama Rau,who is not Diasporic in the true sense but possesses Diasporic sensibility and experience which can be seen in her fiction. Though she has a rich experience of writing autobiography, travelogue, fiction and drama, at present, we shall dwell on her two novels; *Remember the House* and *The Adventures*. *Remember the House* is her first novel which is planned to project the issue of gender and identity; whenever we talk of gender, the question of feminine gender comes up and identity of this particular gender is at stake—over the years. The protagonist of the novel is Ms. Indira Goray who is caught in confusion of almost contradictory cultures, for the simple reason that she has all the makings of a snobbish Indian girl educated in England. After her education in the West when she comes back to Bombay, she gets bored with her snobbish life in the circle of the Westernized families. Initially she develops dislike for the traditional life of Bombay and now it takes the other way round. Her friend-circle includes the Westernized Indians like Jay, Prince of Kalipur, Pria Bhatt and her fiancé Karan Desai and Hari Joshi, too. All these friends are Indians with superficial Western influence and affiliation. She has another set of friends' flex and Nichols who are American couple with fascination towards Indian culture, though they develop occasional repulsions also. These two sets of friends symbolize two sections of the globe with different mental set-up and contradictory views and Indira is caught in between the two. The problem is that of the problem of choice, where to dwell and which are to abandon. So far her lifestyle is that of an amphibian, relying on both, the Western and the Eastern, the native and the alien. Indira also called Baba, has the Western vices of gambling horse-riding and attending parties like Christmas and New Years' Eve, at the same time, she has not disowned her Indianness; evidently the exigencies of life has compelled her to be half-Indian and half Western. After her early careless life, pragmatic sensibility is awakened in him and now she is in search of her true identity out of practical wisdom. She yearns to get over confusion and define the destination of her life. While passing through the stage of observation to that of actual participation she has to undergo all the inconveniences and embarrassments which an individual's experiences in such hours; for instance, when she is publicly kissed by Nichols after swimming; she dislikes it though she is Westernized. We can witness her shyness and embarrassment which reflects her Indian bearings in her mind:

> All the day I carried a certain atmosphere with me hard to describe but quickly committed to people I was with... . All this, I though, for a kiss, power that one has or can generate. (117)

Such experience gives her a jolt. Another complicacy is the idea of marriage because she does not have clear concept of husband or the man she would have in life; and this is seen in the proposal of Hari Joshi:

> Why should we get married? —
> Surely there should be something else?
> ... I think I should be more to
> life than just settling down. I wish
> I know how to explain. (127-8)

The problem is resolved at Chennur, her mother's place, where she falls in love with Krishna and fascinated by his intellectual curiosity and interrogative spirit; for Baba, Krishna is a typical Indian husband; but her dream is shattered when she learns that he is going to be married to another girl at Madras. After the death of her father, she decides to have her own life:

> I think I know the terms in which my life must be lived and that is something. (226)

Now she proposes to Hari, though she is not romantic about marriage:

> Hari, do you still want to marry me, because if you do want to—I'm not in love with you, if that's what you mean though I am not sure what that means." (229)

The author has tried to show how an Indian girl suffers in the process of undergoing deculturation that is, forgetting the Indian values, at least, partially because of her stay and schooling in England, acculturation, that is, being attracted towards the Western lifestyle, and reculturation, that is, trying to relearn the Indian values; Baba comes over the difficulties of life by and by, as she accepts the challenges of life. This novel acquaints us with feminine psychology, at the same time, it plans to highlight the dilemma of character, torn between the two cultures, which at times appear to be diagonally opposite to one another, contradictory to one another and in no way, complimentary to one another. Baba is a typical Indian girl who has to suffer because she wants to retain her Indian ethos and values, at the same time, her attraction towards the Western glamour is illusory and bound to collapse – the consequence is confusion and dilemma, doubt and fear, anxiety and repulsion. It is the lot of a Diaspora.

The Adventures is her second novel which is taken to be a woman's search for fulfilment. Kay is the protagonist of the novel who hails from the Philippines and is on her way to USA for pursuing higher studies in art; in between she is trapped in Japan due to Pearl Harbour incident. She is compelled to escape from the exigencies and get back to her pre-planned way of life. Now she is a victim of political incidents, especially the Pearl Harbour, declared as a war criminal and thus there is an encounter between the individual and circumstances, which finally enters the realm of higher dilemma.

Now she is insecure and this insecurity is her own invited one; she does not surrender to the government nor does she go for suicide; on the other hand, she resolves to cheat the government by having her declared dead by bribing a neighbour. She prefers to die metaphorically, despite existential difficulties and horrors she resolves to live differently:

> Tokyo subways are so shallow that we could hear the noise of the rails outside. Afterwards, we walked home by circuitous routes, followed by the sound of the fires crackling through the house. Once we had grasped the extent of the bombing, the recurring confusions and fires, the lost houses and the dead, we the mother and I, that is,—decided to kill me too. It was surprisingly easy, there were so many burned, unrecognizable bodies. I charred my papers and passport—quite elated at the thought of doing something. After that, we had only to bribe the fishmonger's wife to turn them into the police, to say she had found them in a pile of rubble, the debris of a burned house. I was dead." (36)

This death is of her own making, and now she is entangled with various men. Trying to disentangle herself, depending upon a number of men for a variety of exigential reasons. She wants to live and have a good artistic career of painting. She does not have the desire of a common woman, that of marriage and motherhood, rather she wants to survive in a world of crumbling values. Yet she cannot live her own life; she owes it to Nobuo who has saved her from Interment camp. Now she wants to free herself from Nobuo. Charles Beaver is another man who is a gross widower and wants Kay as her girl friend; she also rejects her by telling a lie:

> Let's just go on for- however long it is and forget about the rest. Nubuo won't divorce me. He is very Japanese. Like the rest, his greedy for impossible contexts, the kind no one can win. He knows I want to leave him. That's

> enough reason for him. And he knows about you—well not that it's you, but that there's someone. It's not hard to check. I tell him that I'm working. He can't argue because he couldn't afford to help his mother, and he's glad that I don't ask him for money. Mostly we live in a terrible silence. I think the silence will only be broken when he wants to marry someone else. (56)

Thus Kay disentangles herself from Charles and then with the help of Colonel Peterson escapes to Manila where she meets Jeremy Wilson, an Air Force Officer flying for the Civil Air Transport. This friendship is, again to escape from Manila to Shanghai; Kay proposes and they are married. Now she has taken the pseudonym of Caterina Gomez and flies to Shanghai under the guise of Mrs. Wilson. This mock-marriage has served her purpose of entering Japan safely. She wants to get Wilson in touch with David, a leading smuggler but Wilson does not agree to this proposal. To liberate herself from the bond of marriage she wants divorce. She again tells a lie to get divorce and thereafter she runs to David with whom she goes to America the land of her final dream. Like an international gipsy she flies from Japan to the Philippines to Shanghai to America. She has to sacrifice the traditional feminism ideals like sexual purity, sacred marriage and motherhood to get her end. She is a stark realist and does not believe in idealistic morality; she is simply an open-hearted opportunist who does not mind speaking sweet lies; she is too practical to believe in morality. Her life is snobbish and superficial without any elemental quality. Obviously the authoress has planned to create a character of Diasporic complexity; the victim of alien culture and politics who has to do all sort of things just to save herself from the uninvited hounding attacks from different corners of the world; this may be taken as the pursuit of a lonely girl, for a home, a shelter, a peaceful life and nowhere she is able to find any of these—this is the tragedy of a feminine gender in search of fulfilment in an alien land.

Let us take Meena Alexander for our nest venture because she is a true Indian Diaspora writer with sincere concern for the Indian soil. We may take her *Fault Lines* published in 1993, a nice memoir-cum-fiction which vibrates with touching memoirs flowing through poetic images, sharp socio-political analysis merging in deep philosophic reflections, as Meena, the person and the persona, strains her every nerve to relate her Indian childhood, African adolescence, British university life, and American present to answer the invariable query in every glob trotting cultural refugee's transnational hybrid mind. Meena Alexander poses a few questions:

> Who are we?
>
> What selves can we construct to live by?
>
> How shall we mark out space ?(174)
>
> What is there to drop back: inside/outside, mind/body, East/West. (20)

The whole work moves with the help of memory which takes the Indian American narrator back to her ancestral Tiruvella House, in far away Kerala, which is a house of emotional bonds, a soothing shelter to her wondering mind, the mind which is cut adrift if not way lost in country thoughts, experiences and realizations. She remembers her childhood days, those magical moments of elation. Undoubtedly, to an Indian, an ancestral house stands for an institution that roots one not merely geographical site, but to a life way, oriented to value system believed in and lived by people through generations. For Meena, her Indian cultural heritage is too precarious to sit her on to a steady life way and life view. As an outsider, she interprets the Indian history and tradition with her West-trained outlook, as 'the other'.

> After all my life did not fall into the narratives I had been taught to honour, takes that close back on themselves, swallowing its own ending, birth, an appropriate education ... an arranged marriage to a man of suitable birth and background somewhere in India. (2)

Meena cherishes to highlight her psychic resistance to the life, ways and customs accepted and appreciated by her ancestors including her own parents, though her parents stayed abroad for years and had exposer to other cultures too, yet there is a distinct difference in the thought pattern of the two generations. Her Sudan experience is noteworthy as she could experience the 'other' and as an 'expatriate Indian child' too distant and different to share the Sudanese ordeals. In a foreign land she had to develop fluency in the high pedigree British English as a mode of survival. This foreign language English alienated her not only from the Sudanese young folk but also from her mother a tongue, the language of the rich culture of her ancestors. She says:

> As I became a teenager, I realized the forked power in the tongue I had acquired: English alienated me from what I was born to. (116)

Alienation is a common trait of Diaspora population and a writer has to keep it in his mind while planning any work like that; Meena has a mixed reaction to the alienation. Regarding mother tongue, she tries to rationalize her refusal to learn the Malayalam script, an 'exclusionary canonical language' to face up 'to the hierarchies of a traditional society', at other times she endorses that her vernacular stores the ancestral wealth of wisdom which sustains her ancestral community; this is her ambiguous stand:

> Why would I ever ... turn those words of the language where I lived and moved my inmost being into English that could never carry that emotion, that would only distant it. (121)

In England, she was made to be conscious of her entity:

> What she actually was, a female from the third world, with no discernible history. (141)

In the West the impression of a woman from India is that of inherent inferiority which is not so in Sudan. She has to face persistent assault, on her 'human dignity' identity and sense which made her violent from within. She decided to break away from her Dutch fiancé, though she cultivated ease with the Western ways and taste.

Now she is in her adopted nation with her Euro-American husband and she as Indian American wife finds it hard to orient herself to the adopted life pattern:

> I did not understand what it meant to keep house in this inconstant fashion, to hold on, to keep going. Often I did not recognize myself, I felt I had lost my soul: that it was sucked by into the vortex of an otherness I had no words for. (104)

Living in US gives an entirely different experience; it is the experience transnational exchange in global trade and digital culture, so to say:

> the old nations of exile, that high estate are gone; smashed underfoot in the transit lounges, in supermarkets, video parlours of the world History maquillage. No homeland here. (193)

How she has learnt that she is a person with multiple cultural anchorages, and in every respect hyphenated:

> Everything that comes to me is hyphenated. A woman poet, a woman poet of colour, a South Indian woman poet who makes up lines in English, a postcolonial language. A third world woman poet, who takes as her right the inner city of Manhattan. (193)

In the alien land, the tussle between the Indian and the American continues, and even her first child can sense it:

> I was growing tense. What did my first born wish for himself? Some nothingness, some transitory zones where dreams roamed, a border country without passport or language. (172)

Meena has become multicultural but the identity of her son is under question and she feels disturbed over the socio-cultural anchorage of her son. She craves neither for India nor for U.S. but a homeland which must be:

> ... touched by hierarchy and authority, and the great weight of centuries... dazzling quickness, its breathless exhilaration ... after all for such as we are the territories are not free. The world is not open. The endless space ... is worse than a lie. (199)

Surprisingly, the memoir ends where it began, but the soul searching furies of Meena remain unresolved:

> Night after night, I asked myself the question, what might it mean to look at myself straight ...? How many different gazes would that need? ...what could one ever be but a mass of fault, a woman cracked by multiple migrations. Uprooted so many times she can connect nothing with nothing, (2-3)

The story of the second generation of Indian American is slightly different as we find in the story of Amita Vasudeva titled 'Journal Entry' collected in the anthology *Our Feet Walk the Sky* published in 1993. Actually she is a cultural refugee, born and grown up in the heart of America, but does not narrate her heritage, rather explores the fear of the children of ethnic descent in the U.S., the fear of being not accepted, being cast off, ignored and ridiculed. She ignores the idea of being 'different':

> Passing. I guess I've always pretty much passed as white. Not white in the colour, white in culture-outwardly only. Why was it so easy to pass? Because I made an effort not to deny or refute any assumptions people had about me. I never really talked about my heritage when young.

This is how the story begins with a strong sense of heritage and that of being overlooked as different. This difference gives her identity both in America and India and this is a new identity she has earned and so she says:

> I prefer to be recognized as distinct from the white bland mass of non-colour and homogeneity that surrounds me. I hate it when people, especially recent Indian immigrants think of me as a totally assimilated American because I'm not- and I don't make any claims to be.

The central character of the story is a multicultural American, who describes her cultural composition as:

> There are certain situations where I am completely American and feel natural and comfortable and good about it because after all I was born and raised in the U.S and there are, of course, times at home with my family, or with Indian friends when I can dress Indian, be around Indian people, and feel just as comfortable.

The question which the writer wants to raise is that whether this cultural identity imply being comfortable only, is it out of one's choice that he adopts another culture and becomes multicultural at his own discretion depending upon the demand of the circumstances, and so she concludes, 'I'm being what I'm.' And this is bold assertion of the writer of the second generation of Indian-American range. The writer's sensitive response to the cultural situation of the new generation is that of multicultural life of America as a situation in multidimensional otherness due to language, life style, rituals, etc. It brings cultural alienation, language alienation and alienation of all sorts, including the severe problem of identity crisis. So the plan of there writers is clandestine, that is, to bring out the problem of identity and alienation due to cultural conflict.

In the world of Indian Diaspora writers, we should not forget Jhumpa Lahiri well known for *Interpreter of Maladies, The Namesake* and *Unaccustomed Earth.* All these works have the theme of Indian immigrant experience in America/Boston, the clash of lifestyles, cultural disorientation, the conflict of assimilation, identity and acculturisation, precisely, the challenges of immigration and exile.

Let us take her recent work, that is, *Unaccustomed Earth,* where she goes for highly qualified and professionally successful Indian Americans with their aching loneliness as an outsider in a foreign land. Truly speaking it is a continuation of her first work, that is, *Interpreter of Maladies.* She takes up the middle class Bengali families or individuals in suburban or campus US, narrated by children or adults who have grown up outside India, so the problem is that of assimilation experienced by the children who are not ready to accept the stereotype traditional life style of the ancestral heritage, rather prefer the latest American way of life. Let us take the five stories of the first section of the book which can be said to be self-contained. 'Unaccustomed Earth', the title story, is about a retired Bengali father, recently widowed who happens to visit his daughter Ruma in Seattle. Ruma has become a mother herself and is yet to recover the jolt that she has got out of her mother's death. The father harbours a secret in his heart, that of a new found love, a Bengali woman, Mrs. Meenakshi Bagchi but he cannot share this secret to his daughter because of the distance between the two:

> He did not want to be part of another family, part of the mess, the feuds, the demands, the energy of it. He did not want to live in the margins of his daughter's life, in the shadow of her marriage. He did not want to live again in an enormous house that would only fill up with things over the years, as the children grew, all the things he'd recently gotten rid off, all the books and papers and clothes and objects are felt compelled to possess, to save. (53)

A sense of nostalgia grips the mind of Ruma's father as he finds his grandson turning his back on his parents because he had also done the same during his childhood; it was inevitable; in the name of ambition and accomplishment he had turned to America deserting his parents and this sense of loss was overwhelming. In the second story 'Hell-Heaven' Usha, the narrator of the story, is a Bengali American who never paid attention to the secret love of her mother towards a regular family visitor Pranab Kaku; she is also betrayed by a man whom she had proposed for marriage. There is difference between the attitude of the mother and the attitude of the daughter towards life:

> ...she had accepted the fact that I was not only her daughter but a child of America as well.(81-82)

'A Choice of Accommodations' is the third story of the second generation of a Bengali immigrant named Amit Sankar who attempts to turn his friend Pam's wedding into a romantic get-away with his wife Magan. She has a doubt that he was having affair with Pam during his academic days at Longford; though Amit refutes the charges, she admits of his having a crush on Pam. Thus the couple fails to develop trust for each other in their conjugal life and become disastrous. 'Only Goodness' in the fourth story of the book, with a theme of failed relationship between a brother and a sister.

Sudha is the elder sister, and Rahul her brother. Initially Sudha introduces Rahul to alcoholism and later on wants to get rid of the ill habit. Sudha's endeavour is to give American upbringing to her brother. She moves to London to study Economics and marries an Englishman who is much older than her age. For the time being Rahul disappears from the scene for no obvious reason; he writes to Sudha after a few years and Sudha invites him to London. Sudha suffers from the sense of guilt of initiating her brother into alcoholism which proves disastrous as she has to kick him out, finally, out of her house. The last story of the first section of the book is 'Nobody's Business' which is also about a Bengali immigrant lady, named Sangeeta Biswas or Sang. She lives with Paul and Heather, her room-mates and gets regular proposal for marriage by suitors even by Paul. However, she doesn't accept any offer and goes for the love of her own choice, an Egyptian named Freddy and it meets a disastrous end with the entry of Derrida Frain, a second woman in his life. Evidently, all the five stories of the first section have disastrous ending with a different message that the writer plans to propagate, a common happening with any Diasporic entity, an Indian living abroad, man or woman, child or adult, everyone is in the Diasporic dilemma of existence on the whole of self and solves.

The book *Unaccustomed Earth* has a second section titled 'Hema and Kaushik' which contains three stories which are interlinked and deals with loss and love, revolving around two people Hema and Kaushik, children of two different Bengali families thrown together, on and off across the years, by the accident of immigration; it may be taken as a triology. The first story of the triology is narrated by Hema where she describes a farewell party arranged for Kaushik and his family when they left for India; thereafter the two families lost contact. One morning Dr. Choudhuri, Kaushik's father, calls up and informs that they are returning to Massachusetts and would like to stay with Hema's family, till they find a house and this return brings the two families together, particularly Hema and Kaushik. The second story is titled 'Year's End,' which is narrated by Kaushik:

> I did not attend my father's wedding. I did not even know there had been a wedding until my father called early one Sunday during my final years at Swarthmore. (252)

Here the gap between the relationship of father and son is visible. It also reveals the tragic homecoming of Kaushik to Massachusetts house where his beloved mother Parul had lived before succumbing to cancer. His father had married again with Chitra, a mother of two daughters, the daughters who have shifted to new city and forced to accept a replacement for a dead parent like Kaushik. The third part of the triology is narrated by Hema, an omniscient narrator; it is set in Rome where Hema and Kaushik meet again, decades after their early meeting. In fact, Kaushik has travelled across continents as a photo journalist and Hema is on the look out for the last vestiges of Etruscan culture. Thereafter, Kaushik moves to Hong Kong to join his new job of a photo editor for an international news magazine and Hema goes back to India to get married to Navin, a Professor of Physics at Michigan State. At the lunch hour at Paola's house they meet and instantly relate to each other. Kaushik proposes to her but she refuses and Kaushik ends his life by drawing himself at Hong Kong. This triology is like a moving novella which ends in a sense of waste of love and loss of life.

Lahiri's plan in *Unascertained Earth* is to present characters with insight, sense of loss they feel for being uprooted from their culture, a strong nostalgia, emotional integration with their new country as well as the old ones, the feeling of inside-outsider and cultural displacement. The epigraph of *Unaccustomed Earth* summarises all:

> Human nature will not flourish ... if it be planted and replanted, for too long a series of generations, in the same worn-out soil. My children ... shall strike their roots into unaccustomed earth. (Extracted from Nathanid Hawthorne's *The Custom House*)

The most remarkable fact to be noticed in the book is Lahiri's depiction of gulf that separates the immigrant not only from their homelands, but from their own flesh and blood; that is, the parents from their children, first generation from second generation and likewise; while parents try to retain their Indianness even in America their children feel home in America and the little Indians do not matter to them; this, on the other hand, creates tensions and communication gaps. Precisely, the complexity is regarding cultural assimilation more sincerely; straddling between two cultures they are unable to accept anyone heartily and fully. The characters are emotionally outsiders and suffer loss, that of, a parent, a partner, a brother or an ideal while moving across cultures; Lahiri wishes to establish their identity in the hounding space of menace and anguish, a fresh recipe tabled before the readers and audience.

The above quoted writers and their work establish the fact that there is a definite plan behind the set up, that is, the creativity is with an intention to focus the Diaspora sensibility.

Works Cited

Alexander, Meena, *Fault Lines: A Memoir*, New York: The Feminist Press, 1993.

Desai, Anita, *Bye-Bye Blackbird,* New Delhi, Orient Paperbacks, 1985.

Jasbir, Jain, "The Use of Fantasy in the Novels of Anita Desai", in *Explorations in Modern Indo-English Fiction,* New Delhi: Bahri Pub., 1992.

Lahiri, Jhumpa, *Unaccustomed Earth*, New Delhi: Random House India, 2000.

Mistry, Rohinton, *Such a Long Journey*, New Delhi: Rupa & Co., 1991.

Rau, S.R., *Remember the House*, London: Victor Golanc, 1956.

____ *The Adventures,* New Delhi: Hind Pocket Books, 1973.

Vasudevan, A., "Journal Entry in *Our Feet Walk the Sky*, (Ed.), *The Women of South Asian Descent Collective*, San Franscisco:" Aunt Lute Books, 1993.

5

Difference from the Stay-at-Homes

So far we have analyzed the works of Indian Diaspora writers and come to know their main trends of writing, their theme, their characters and their mind/plan behind writing fiction. We have a good number of Indian English writers who cannot be termed as Indian Diaspora writers, rather they may be termed as writers stay-at-home. In this chapter the planning is to diagnose the difference between the writings of the writers staying at home and the writers called Diaspora writers in various exigencies, say, their approach, selection of theme, style, characterization, etc.

Indian English writers have developed their own corpus of writing out of an unswerving faith and hope, myths and traditions, customs and rites. As K.R. Srinivas Iynger points out:

> English has became ours, it is not less ours for being primarily the English man's or American's and Indo Anglian literature too is our literature, the literature which, with all its limitations, still taught us to be a new nation and a new people. (8)

Let us take the trio first, the trio of R.K. Narayan, M.R. Anand and Raja Rao, who are supposed to be the pillars of Indian English fiction.

Let us review R.K. Narayan's *The Guide,* the Sahitya Akademi Award winning novel, for its artistic excellence and popular appeal. *The Guide*, despite all adverse comments, dwells on the traditional Indian soil with its superstition belief, taboo and exigencies of Indian life. William Walsh is of the view that Narayan's is a fastidious art which blends realism poetry, melancholy, perception and gaiety; it fuses self-affirming sincerity and a self negating irony. It is packed, lucid, beautifully organized and deeply Indian novel. It is also taken as Raju's odyssey where the runaway sinner turns a saint and meets a poignant end where as Raju-Rosie relationship, better call it friendship, remains a central paradox, bringing crisis in the novel in different phases of life. The meeting of Raju and Rosie marks a turning point in the life of the three, Raju, Rosie and Marco. Marco is basically a cerebral man occupied with historical research amidst caves and ruins and incapable of understanding, much less satisfying, the physical urges and emotional aspirations of his talented wife Rosie, a Devdasi, by birth and upbringing. Naturally, she has a passion for dance in her blood where she can derive her heart's joy and fulfilment. Her married life has made her a caged bird with suppressed instinct for freedom, spontaneity and self-expression. Raju appears as a saviour and beckons her light to release from the dark tunnel; finally, he resorts to risk a mother's separation and society's castigation to dedicate himself completely to fill the loveless and cheerless void of her life. It is also an escape for him from his dull routine activities.

With Raju's sustained publicity campaign and astute managerial skill, Rosie's talent gets accomplishment and recognition; with reputation comes money, palacial residence and a regular musician's troupe; Rosie is now an established figure, a star attraction and Raju becomes the master of establishment. This affluence and grandeur of glamour brings in the ill habits of alcoholism, gambling, etc. He begins to squander his new found fortune, fixes Rosie's dance at a relentless pace, accepts undue advances, etc. Such showmanship, fanfare and unremitting exertion begins to tell upon the personal and intimate bond between the lovers. Rosie comes to know the historical achievement of her husband Marco, his published book and Raju's endeavour to hide it. She is stunned to see the arrest warrant of Raju charging him with forging her signature to claim her jewellery box. Despite her best efforts Raju is jailed, and this is final:

> If I have to pawn my last possession, I'll do it to save you from jail. But once it's over, leave me once for all; that's all I ask. Forget me. Leave me to live or die, as I choose; that's all. (198)

Thus the relationship is strained and Rosie leaves for Madras never to return. On the other hand, Raju, after release from prison, strays into a village temple and is regarded as a swami. Not only that, he gets involved with people's faith until he almost gets killed through keeping a twelve-day fast to invoke the rain gods in a drought-stricken land.

This is a typical Indian English novel which has nothing to do with the theme of Indian English Diaspora fiction. The plot is that of Indian soil and Indian culture, the meeting, the dissociation, the rift in marriage, realization, reunion, superstition—all are pure Indian; there is no conflict or crisis of the Diaspora fiction. We should examine the circumstantial and psychological base of the crisis that precipitates in the lover's separation. It is not that Raju is an unmitigated crook or Rosie is an absolute crank; at least their thinking and conduct do not vindicate so. We also trace the elements of individuality and eccentricity, flexibility and adjustment for understanding are another. When Raju stakes his familial and social values in his fellowship with a dancing girl and faces adversaries for Rosie's sake, the main impulse was not self-pleasure and self-advancement; even his concealment of Marco's book and the forgery incident were more acts of folly than knavery, of indiscretion than perjury; his compulsive urge was to posses Rosie's love all for himself, and not her wealth and jewellery by dumping her. On the other hand, Rosie is not always inflexible nor steadfastly stubborn. She does not accurse Raju of treachery and betrayal even in the worst moment of crisis, "I felt all along you were not doing right things. This is Karma" (193).

Rosie applies herself unremittingly to work in order to raise finances for the bail bond and for his defence. Surprisingly, she contemplates a suicide pact desiring to die together and make a united exit from an unkind world. There was no essential incompatibility in their tastes and temperaments such as it was between Marco and Rosie. Finally, the barrier between the two lovers is dissolved and the channel of understanding closed for ever. Rosie's announcement that she wasn't havig any relationship with Raju is a reversal, as if she disowns her own self. In the final stage, a rupture develops between the two lovers which appears to be contrived and does not strike as a natural culmination of a process consistent with the nuances of their characterization portrayed penetratingly but they never talk of marriage. Both the characters have positive potential and it is visible when they abandon Malgudi for Mangala and Madras, taking care of circumstances and not individuals. In his *My Dateless Diary*, Narayan writes:

> I have the whole picture ready in my mind ... the only question is to put it in writing. ...I have on my hands the life of a man condemned to death before he was born and grown, and I have to plan my narrative to lead to it. (105-6)

In the first part of the novel the characters took change of the circumstances in working out their destinies, in the second part the author consciously fit them in a pre-determined pattern which can be said to be a deflection and not a development. The characters are unsure of their destination; they are unable to rediscover the resources of their love, and their escapades into Mangala and Madras are a turning away from life and from their own selves, and the central dilemma is left far behind. It is noteworthy that the past is delinked and the characters are left apart to begin all over again.

Initially these characters have a self generated vitality to struggle through the labyrinth of passion and the challenge of circumstances. Later on they lose their verve and dynamism and resign to their destiny.

Raju, as a reluctant holy man, is caught up with public adulation and engrossed in keeping up appearances but there is no serious attempt at self-examination or introspection, no serious probe into his weaknesses and lapses.

Consequently, his holiness is not evolved out of an inmate yearning for a better life, and his conversion is induced by extraneous factors. His threat of fasting is a bogus which cannot defuse quarrels and ironically boomerang upon him into real hunger penance to propitiate the rain gods for the prosperity of the land.

Rosie has started a new life, yet her life carries a strong imprint of Raju: "She had settled down at Madras and was looking after herself quite well."

Her creativity ceases and she is restless as before:

> I'm tired of all this circus existence. It was your own choice. Not the circus life. I visualized it as something different. It's all gone with that old home of yours. (198)

Such denouncement has nothing to do with the crisis at Malgudi, a totally different context; the characters fail to attend transcendence and proper grounding for renewal. Truly speaking, renunciation without sacrifice is abandonment of struggle, ascetism without control is a running away from life's problems. The novel ends mysteriously with no answer to rain, Raju's life, or Rosie's future. Such is the creation of an Indian English writer who cannot be bracketed under 'Diasporas' but entirely different in plot, situation and characterization.

William Walsh in his study of R.K. Narayan strikes his writing for its range of situation, incisive perception, rich variety of characters, the inimitable unbreakable rhythm of feeling, intelligence and life, coherent and inclusive vision and its subdued poetic style. In fact, Narayan applies the local, micro level constituent units placing it within the relevant tradition which, at times, appear to be an original blend of Western method and Eastern material. The minute fidelity with which the surface of Malgudi life is effortlessly reproduced, the streets, the houses, the shops, the temples, the trades, the routines and crises of the family, the exact grain and patina of place and people, Malgudi becomes for Walsh not only a metephor of India but also a metaphor for everywhere. A balance is maintained between the individual and the universal character in the ideological and discursive location. In Narayan's text the struggle for survival and ascendancy in a field marked by colonial and neo-colonial hegemony is conveniently overlooked but its tendency is to essentialise Indian identity, and its treatment of gender, class and caste are all superseded on the individual and his quest for universal moral meaning. Consequently the text as the object of a moral discourse claims universality for its imperatives, the discursivities underlying the construction of texts.

Unlike the Diaspora writers, Narayan uses of the technique of employing subtler, almost hidden use of Hindu mythology and philosophy. His human comedies are woven around a complex web of Indian metaphysical traditions and gather deeper significance when understood against this background. One critic, Viney Kripal, for instance, elaborates Raju's *(The Guide)* experience of the world as the archetypal four stage journey, as laid down in the *Dharma Shastra*, in order to attain salvation. Childhood student, householder, hermit or recluse, and the ascetic. Raju overcomes his fellies and misfortunes to become a true saint by the end of the novel. It may be called as dialectic of *Maya* or the illegalization of *Maya* which is of central importance to Indian literature. Rosie is an embodiment of this principle, also called an allegorical or symbolic representation of *Maya-nartaki / nartaki-maya* dichotomy whose seductive presence all through the novel imprisons Raju in the illusion of the world. Raju's imprisonment is a sort of Karmic *moksha*. Besides, it represents bourgeois ethics as a spiritual need of the Hindu psyche, as expressed:

> the villagers express ... the need for a spiritual mentor in their midst to lead them to salvation, the only true end. So pervasive is this ideal in the traditional Hindu psyche that every school of Hindu thought emphasizes the importance of a spiritual preceptor, teacher. Raju, only unwittingly fills this need for a guru. (359)

Narayan, himself, makes his intention clear as he says:

> ... passing inevitably, through phases of symbolic, didactic, or over-dramatic writing, one arrived at the stag of valuing realism, psychological explanations, and technical virtuosity. The effort was interesting, but one had to differ from one's models in various ways. In an English novel, for instance, the theme of romance is based on a totally

> different conception of man-woman relationship from ours... And the hold of religion and the conception of gods ingrained in us must necessarily find a place in any accurate portrayal of life. (122-23)

Here the thematic is the realist mode of the English novel whereas the problematic is the accurate portrayal of India. It shows the image of the nation, the India of sages, of non-violence, of marriages made in heaven, of the join family and of godly or demoniac proportions of actions and reactions set in limitless worlds. Not only that, here, resistance becomes an insistence on an origin and teleological identity, hybridity and heterogeneity become its contingent causalities. All these things become more vivid when we go through Narayan's *The Man Eater of Malgudi* which is self-consciously Indian as we find explicit references to Hindu mythology, the Bhasmasur legend.

Natraj, the protagonist of the novel, is the owner of a small printing press in the fictional town of Malgudi who encounters with Vasu, an eccentric stranger, basically, a taxidermist. Vasu's sudden intrusion disturbs the placid world of Natraj and turns it topsy-turvy. Narayan projects the dichotomy between Vasu and Natraj: Vasu, an arrogant and brash personality, Natraj, a peace-loving and compromising person. The stage is set for the calm sage at peace with himself versus the brazen but restless demon. Now the demon is to be destroyed so that the cosmic order can be maintained.

Natraj's printing press is the central trope, a metonymic site towards an originary subjectively, with a topography of a temple, mirroring the inner and outer sanctums, Vasu's rough encroachment is disliked and resented; on the other hand, the press also symbolizes modernity and progress. The two have unequivocal relationship. Vasu is destroyed in classical Hindu fashion, through the agency of Moga, the female dancer of the temple Rangi, who is a town prostitute also. Natraj assistant Sastri sums up the whole episode:

> every demon appears in the world with a special boon of indestructibility. Yet the universe has survived all The *rakshasas* that were ever born every demon carries within him, unknown to himself, a tiny seed of self destruction,

> and goes up in the air at the most unexpected moment. Otherwise what is to happen to humanity? (182-83)

In this novel, Narayan has given an account of Hinduism and its recuperative capabilities. His vision in the novel stresses on realist framework to bolster a tradition of national authority, and constructs a native temporarily which describes uniquely Indian days in the detail of its passing time. Malgudi days evoke national peculiarities like Natraj's daily visit to the river for a bath early in the morning at exactly the same time as the opening and closing time of the press, or Chandran's regular evening visit to the river in 'The Bachelor of Arts' or even Raju waiting for tourists at the railway station. Precisely Malgudi becomes a chronoscope, in which national time becomes concrete and visible. Narayan's evocation of Malgudi and its little idiosyncrasies deliberately evoke timeless antiquity and tradition. Defying diverse interpretations of the novel, the elaborate rendition of the traditional Hindu world-view and its resourcefulness in terms of resisting the incursions of the other dominant cultures. Besides its deceptive simple form, the novel is informed by a complex network of Hindu thought and traditions and sets up the dichotomies of the weak and the strong, good and evil, average and extraordinary, ancient and modern, passive and religious, the *rishi* and the *raskshasa,* etc. Thus the totalizing impulse of the nation subsumes the diverse struggle of people across different historical times of India which has multicultural social and political environment. Such elaborations are completely absent in Diaspora writings.

Another most important writer to be discussed under head is Raja Rao whose early phase is certainly not Diasporic. His works are so deeply immersed in Indian tradition and culture that he may be categorized as an English writer with a high influence of the *Vedas*, *Upanishads* and all Hindu scriptures, for whom 'the tradition is so alive' in India. Consequently' *Sruti, Smriti and Achana* have been referred enormously in *The Serpent and the Rope*. He makes mention of rituals, practices and the popular culture of legends and tales; all these exist in a state of simultaneity in the Indian mind, its tradition, present in Indian psyche, as he defines:

> Civilization is nothing but the familiarity with which we go into the inner property, cultivated and manured from age to age. The rivers have washed alluvial soil to it and the rains have poured and gcne down into the sea, and brought back as it were, the perfume of the same land; so that when our mangoes fall and we eat, we know it is the product of a thousand years. (90)

In the novel, for Ramaswamy, life is a pilgrimage and he wants to know all about the sacred places, their significance, etc. He finds himself to be an orphan till he is ignorant of these places, "Some deep absence which neither love nor learning could fulfill." (26)

Like any pure and innocent sole contain questions come to his mind:

> Who am I? And who are you? What is the place from which I came? Who is my mother? Who is my sire? Pondering thus, perceive them all as fancies only without substance. Give up the world as an idle dream.

He has to face the fact that has given importance to unimportant things; he has to become *dhira* of the *Upanishads* and seek the meaning of the Ultimate which is only possible when one can distinguish the real from the unreal, rooted steadfast in knowledge that the awful serpent is but the innocent rope, negating what the *Vedanta* calls the illusion of the world while affirming the underlying reality of Brahman. Ramaswamy confronts the fact of human condition when he concludes:

> existence is a passage between life and death, and birth and death again, and what an accumulation of pain man has to bear? Is it then a wonder the Buddha, with palaces and queens, with a kingdom and heir, left his home to find an that from which there is no returning? You could only live in life, and to what that means is to know the whole of wisdom. (135)

Since he is a Brahmin, he strives to go beyond history to shuttle in time and to take the accumulated wisdom by horns as it were. He cannot ignore the imperative with a sage to begin the genealogical tree; he should seek a guru to end the cycle of birth and death and he has to do it. Raja's work is replete with the words of wisdom from the *Vedanta* which is also known as *Adhyatma Shastra* that cannot be combined to a geographic entity, rather it is a principle India is credited with. Obviously, *inanam* is India which is the only nation that has questioned the existence of the world, of the object; once the principle is espoused wherever the *sadhak* is or goes to, he discovers India; he is India; and Raja Rao quotes:

> This body is the holy place Bereaves; land here flows) the all pervasive Ganges of wisdom, the mother of the three worlds; this devotion and this faith are Gaya; the contemplation of the feet of my own preceptor is prayaga; this Inner self, the Brahman, the witness of the mind of all people, is the God, the land of the Universe; if everything (thus) abides in myself, is there any other shine (besides it)? (216)

It is true that the ideal of India is sainthood which can be reached by the extinction of the ego. *Vedanta* makes use of *Karma*, *Jnana* and *Vairagya* in the context of *Jivan-Mukti* and Raja Rao uses them in his works. This is the impact of Indian philosophy which is brought to the fore in isolate existences of India in which India is remembered, experienced and commemorated beyond history as tradition, as the truth (352). C.D. Narasimha in the introduction of *The Serpent and the Rope* calls it an evocation of this truth, the tradition of India and its vitality, especially in its encounter with the West. India is seen as an idea, not as an area on the map.

Another significant aspect of the novel is its reiteration of the feminine principle, otherwise known as womanhood, motherhood, fair sex and an immaculate power behind everything of the world. Raja Rao says in *The Serpent and the Rope:*

> ... woman is the earth, air, ether, sound; woman is the microcosms of the mind, the articulations of the space, the knowing, the knowledge; the woman is fire, movement clear and rapid as the mountain stream; woman is that which seeks against that which is sought. (357)

Rao tells a lot more as a salutation to woman, which may be taken as the chief postulation of Hinduism where God is taken as mother and Shakti; it also suggests the identification of woman with cosmic pulse and vitality, even the kinetic immanent aspect of God. It also leads to the formulation of a concept of consciousness and its power, call it Shiva-Shakti: considered philosophically, Shiva the unchanging consciousness and Shakti its changing power, manifesting itself as mind and matter. The metaphysical quest of Rao's hero is to attain the truth that seems possible only through the realization of the absolute self. In *The Serpent and the Rope* the protagonist Rama says:

> The world is spread for the woman to be, and in making us know the world woman shows that the world is oneself seen as the other. Union is proof that the Truth is non-dual. Man sees himself in woman as essence the fact of womanhood is the meaning of his life—the woman needs our worship for her fulfilment, for in worshipping her we know the world and annihilate it, absorbing it into ourselves. (172-174)

The affairs of Rama with women are not only affirmation of sex but also recognition as essence and meaning of life, as the visual beauty of truth, faith, love and endurance. He learns to accept the connotations of co-existence of sexes in the divine person, as integration of two principles, energy and spirit, and so he says:

> A man's world have led all of us, one by one, to the top of Himalaya; and like the Cathars, who hated mating and the making of children, we would have taken consolamentum and flung ourselves over the precipice, singing hymns on the void ... Buddhism died in India because it become ascetic, and so denied womanhood its right to exist. Those who hate woman—must end themselves, as the cathars Did, fasting unto death. (172)

When Rama meets Saroja, his sister, his feminine impulse is awakened and he accepts it:

> ... was a strange sensation to me—that Saroja was my sister made the knowledge of her womanhood natural to

> me—natural to see, to observe and even to breathe ... I felt that maturity in a girl was like new moon or the change of equinox, it had polar affinities ... there was, too, a feeling of temple sanctuary and I would now understand why primitive people took the first blood of menstruation for the better harvesting of their fields. And why Indian gave such beautiful names to their woman—what a deep and reverential mystery womanhood is I would bow before Saroja and call her Queen. (52)

Now Rama can sense why he is alienated from his wife Madeline, and know the reason:

> The pure were dear to me. Madeline, too, got involved in them but for a different reason. Touch as I have said, was always distasteful to her, so she liked the untouching Cathars, she loved their celibacy. She enplaned me to practice the ascetic *brahmcharya* of my ancestors and I was too proud a Brahmin to feel defeated. (17)

Madeline suffers from a deficiency and so she is unable to get over her personal loss and for a retreat into a sterile kind of living which can result in a separate metaphysic and loneliness. She becomes a Buddhist and her womanhood is denied. On the other hand, Savithri embodies the feminine principle and sensibility in her surrender to the masculine and the hypostatic presence of Rama which he seeks. This association gives an integral vision and feeling, as he says:

> ... people have asked me—Georges among them- what indeed it was that happened between Savithri and me in Cambridge. Nothing more had happened, in fact, than if you see deep and long at silence you perceive ... which explains why Parvathi is daughter of Himalaya, and Sita born to the furrow of the field. I heard myself say, I heard myself or I saw my eyes see that I saw. She become the awareness behind my awareness, the leap of my understanding. I lost the world and she became it. For whatever I gave her she accepted as the Ganges receives the waters of Himalayas, that go on down to the sea—so we gave love to each other, as though it did not belong to us, but to a principle, on other, on impersonal reality, from which we saw gifts emerge in each of us, and gave each other with ceremony For us, therefore, all was celebration, festival ... (171-72)

In the novel, the union between Rama and Savithri culminates in a wedding which symbolizes the marriage between Being and power to become the Divine, all presented symbolically by Rao. Thereby we get the concept of *mudras, tattva, sadasiva, mantra, nada, mantric stage, bindu* and *om,* and also that of *Nada Bindu, Gyan Shakti, Brahmi Shakti* (desire), *Kama Shakti* (action or violation) and *Shabda Brahma* in the shape of *Kundalini Shakti*; *Om* is suggestive of the identification of *Kundalini Shakti* with *Shabda Brahma*, the source of all speech. Finally Rama is confronted with the ambiguities and perplexities of knowledge and time, and engages himself in a metaphysical quest for truth which enables him to apprehend man as the juncture of realms of knowledge. For him, the feminine principle becomes vital for judging him of man and matters, philosophic and political systems, an incornational principle, the juncture of the finite with the infinite, of the temporal with the eternal, and with the world as a whole. This is the manifestation of the Indian philosophy to which Rao is adhered to and elaborates it in fair proportion in his works. Indian English Diaspora writings never indulge in such a deep Indian philosophy and never highlights the feminine sensibility in such an exact proportion, and here lies the difference between the two groups of writers, taken together.

However, the extraneous philosophic content of the novel *The Serpent and the Rope* has raised so many questions, central of which is the real intention of the writer. As we explain we find it is the history of an intellectual's quest for self-knowledge which takes the form of memory and autobiography and an affirmation in philosophic terms of universal truths to which the hero is guided by tradition, thinking and experience. Structurally it deals with events in time and space, and celebration of truths transcending these dimensions. The protagonist is deliberately in quest of self-discovery because he is an intellectual with a passion for objectivity, living his life in full consciousness of his intellectual heritage, making his choice deliberately as a responsible individual. The opening of the novel establishes his identity, 'I was born a Brahmin,' and it sums up his career:

> The Brahmin is never contemporary he goes backwards and forwards in time, and so has a sage to begin the genealogical tree, and Guru,to end the cycle of birth and death. (125)

Raja Rao has given an elaborate description of Brahmins and Brahminhood which is the identity of Rama, and the other is his self 'I'. He is both *Jiva* and *Atman* which Rama affirms again and again as *Shivoham, Shivoham* the indistinguishable from the Brahman. It is inheritance by birth but it is, even more significantly, a matter of deliberate choice. Rao says:

> He indeed the Brahmin who turns the crest inward... the true life, the true Brahmin hood commençes when you recognize yourself in your eternity. At some moment you must stop life and look into it... And as you go on dipping and rising in your inner Ganges ... you undo your knots. (216)

The decision of Rama 'to a life and look into it' brings about everything that happens in *The Serpent and the Rope*, for him self-recognition is of utmost importance and no achievement can compete with it:

> Never can you escape eternity, for never can you escape that "I" even when you say you can, it is the "I" saying it. Can the "I" say anything? No, it cannot no more than eternity can be seen in time. But time seeing itself is eternity, just as waveseeing itself is water ... (215)

Significantly, the epigraph chosen from Atmananda Guru makes things more clear: "waves are nothing but water. So is the sea."

This novel has the presence of India in its totality, for instance, family relationships, rituals, the atmosphere of places like Hyderabad, Bangalore, Bombay and Allahabad, Indian symbols like the Himalaya, Kashi and Ganga, and as a vivid truth.

For Rama, India remains a symbol of knowledge which transcends time and help him fight spiritual barrenness. Rao's formulation is clandestine:

> The world is either unreal or real- the serpentor the rope. There is no in-between-the-two and all that's in-between is poetry, is sainthood. (315)

His journey of self-recognition is an inward journey and it does not end with Savithri; he has evil traits, that is, the ego as the source of suffering which can be removed with the help of a Guru only, and he finds one, rather he discovers one, mysteriously:

> I do not know where I want, but I was happy there for it was free and broad like a sunny day and like a single broad river it was. I had reached Benaras- Benaras. I had risen from the Ganges, and saw the luminous world, my home. I saw the silvery boat, and the boatman had a face I knew. I know his face as one knows one's face in deep sleep. He called me and said, "It is so long, so long my son. I have awaited you. Come, we go. 'I want, and man, I tell you, my brother, my friend, I will not return. I have gone whence' There is no returning ... (403)

Such is the world of Raja Rao and the world of Indian English writing completely divorced from the Indian English Diaspora world.

Another important signature in the Indian English writing is that of Mulk Raj Anand for whom the novel is a vehicle for conveying his deepest concern for the human predicament in contemporary India, a weapon of humanism. Let us analyze his triology, also known as 'Lalu' triology and, *Untouchable*, *Coolie* and *The Big Heart*, which speak of India as a whole. Lalu is the protagonist and every man, say, a common man. The readers may trace the origin of his career from the small village community into which he is born, his experience in Flanders with the Indian army and his return back to his homeland. He fights to defend the values that he himself does not believe in and when he comes back he finds his family dead, scattered and lost. He has to involve himself in radical politics exchanging bewilderment for commitment; The change that is chronicle is pivotal to Anand's whole development. He adopts the genuine problems of the soil as the theme of his works, such as, the inadequacies of capitalist government, the traditional fatalism of the peasantry class, the inflexibility of the caste system, etc. All his characters, whether Lalu, or Bakha or Munoo, draw our sympathy and have ulterior desire to escape the social prison. Destiny plays a significant role in their life. Munoo of Coolie is defeated by the system and takes destiny into his own hands when he decides to run away from Babu, though it does not suit his survival trick and dies of tuberculosis. Lalu is apparently stronger because of his varied experience.

Let us take the novel *The Village* as he attempts to portray a common village of India, its rural life and the countryside imperceptibly being modernized, with poverty and diviease as its important ingredient. Lalu does not luxuriate in self-pity and so, in this sense at least, he is unlike Bakha or Munoo; he aspires improvement and development. Though he has a keen eye and a sensitive nose, he resigns to the inevitability of things and so he dislikes the changes, yet he aspires for the brick-houses, and the European luxury. Surprisingly, he does not find any consolation in God but in a hostile deity, "The twilight was falling as if the hand of God was throwing invisible dust into the open eyes of the world." (52)

For him there is a vindictive God and an indifferent one. He finds himself isolated as Bakha and Munoo, and is waiting for a moment of revelation. He becomes a rebel, and defies his Sikh tradition without understanding the consequences of sacrilege which is nothing but assertion of the self and results in kicking him out of society and village though he returns after a long gap. Actually, *The Village* is autobiographical to a great extent. Lalu has a fantasy love for Maya, the landlord's daughter. He is patronized by the European officials, the District Commissioner Herbert Long but his growing objectivity about his own environment is noticeable. Lalu joins the Indian Army and returns when his father is dying, upset at his emotionless ness than at the death itself. He is not like his companion:

> He found himself becoming graver and graver. And he felt he could be no longer the simple crony of Gughi, Ghulam and Churanji. They were running mad for the sheer joy

> of meeting him... Lalu listened with amusement but he felt himself choking with disgust. For though his face was warm with happiness at meeting his friends and walking on the old earth, which blossomed with the promise of new harvest of cotton and sugarcane and millet, he felt that he was now only a passer-by. (225)

Self-enquiry and sophistication bring sadness to the plot; there is lamentation at the loss of innocence. In fact, Anand wants to eradicate poverty, disease and injustice, and for such a noble cause what is required is intelligence, worldliness and idealism, but the gulf between the wish to help, and those who help, between the idealist and the object of ideals is a matter of great concern, and so Lalu bids farewell to his village:

> He felt as if he world break down with the sadness of leaving this land. But though the liquid walled up in his eyes and there was the taste of salt on his tongue, he could not weep and merely sat listening to the rattling wheels of the carriage speeding along through the rich hot shade after sunset. (238)

Lalu could never be an integral part of his village community which had humiliated him abruptly.

Another novel that follows *The Village* is *Across the Black Water*. As the title of the novel suggests Lalu is to cross the seven seas in order to go abroad, that is England, called *Vilayat* in Hindu. It shows a knowledge of the pity and suffering of war that comes as much from isolated impressions which Anand himself received during the Spanish civil war. It is built on fundamental irony of the fact that the men who were herded by the thousands to fight in Europe for the king-emperor were totally unsuited to the modern warfare. Lalu's village has a detailed picture of a community rooted in superstitions and rituals, where the pattern of daily life has become sanctified, routine, scarcely affected by the technological changes introduced by the British government in the opening pages of *The Village*. The father of Lalu is surprised by the train whistle, in the novel *Across the Black Water* as the sepoys arrive in France. Lalu is scared, as he has crossed the sea, the black water, as a victim of superstition:

> As you know, I always laughed at Mullah for saying everything was ordained by God, and mocked at my mother for believing in Fate, and still I don't believe in either, but I tell you one thing—the moment when life meets Death is frightening. (171)

During war the sense of terrible isolation brightens Lalu as he cannot reconcile with any supernatural deity and has confronted death several times.

In *The Village*, Lalu had felt the stirrings of sexual feelings in his idealistic affection for Maya, the daughter of the landlord, but 'Maya' is literally appearance only; in *Across the Black Water* Lalu's sexual desire becomes a real manifestation, the only refuge from the surrounding horrors of war, as a possibility that human love can be briefly reaffirmed amid the bewilderingly unleashed hatred. Lalu and his companions are amazed at the open lifestyle of the West; with a highly conservation background, they find themselves completely disillusioned in this new lifestyle of the West. Particularly Lalu, when he is confronted by the indelicate obviousness of Western sexual overturns, he withdraws into a shell of Indian shyness and bleak despair of traditional pattern:

> Such a contrast to the sedate Indian women who seemed to grow old before they were young, flabby and tired, except for a cowherd women with breasts like pyramidal rocks. (19)—the girl lifted the edge of her skirt to show the naked flesh between her legs and them, with a deliberate 'ooh' dropped it again. Instead of laughing or smiling as the other did, Lalu found himself reduced to an emptiness fro the centre of which his two eyes seemed to see this world as an enormous closure, crowded by hordes of hard, gigantic shapes which were oppressing him. (64-65)

Lalu remains withdrawn, observant and isolated in the whole novel, and other sepoys are deeply engrossed in sensual pleasure and other outwardly pleasures abandoning all rituals and traditions; surprisingly they are horrified to see the battle injury or death. Anand has another cancer: on the one hand battle demands a total submission of personality to the general order and yet, on the other hand, it heightens the individual sense of his own personal doom. In fact, war is fought by armies and suffered by individuals, and it is agonizingly revealed by Lalu. He questions the basis of war which wrecks so many lives:

> The elements of sanity in Lalu persisted in the face of guns and in the face of the insanity which had blown off the towers of the churches, and he could not believe that ordinary men and women of good sense, and the Governments of France, England and Germany, which were saner and wiser than the ordinary people over whom they ruled, could be engaged in a war in which men were being wounded and the houses shattered. (104)

In the novel *The Village* Lalu is isolated from society and in this novel, the devastating effect of war is presented. Anand has tried to highlight the defects of the normal Indian society through his description of war, for instance, it presupposes the absolute authority of the elite, the irrevocability of hierarchy. And the necessity for those at the foot of the pyramid to slave and suffer for the efficient working of the overall system. In this novel the author communicates the claustrophobic tension of men in the front line, the immanence of death and the pervading sense of inevitability which is the root of so much Indian friction. In war, men fight for one incentive only: there is a complete absence of soul-commitment; loss of faith becomes overt, sleep and waking, dream and reality, are confused in the front line trenches; only one reality persists and this is the necessity to save oneself, not to lose the last shred of identity in the impersonality of battle. Lalu fears the encroaching negation of individuality. Thus the novel can be categorized as highly pessimistic, as Lalu is taken prisoner. It is the only novel of its kind in which the plight of the ordinary man is more desolate, directed towards death, mutilation, continuous battle and nothing else.

The Sword and the Sickle is the last part of the trilogy. The title is highly symbolic: the sickle is the vast mass of India's labour force, call them peasants, the untouchables, etc., and the sword is that force which seeks perpetually to subjugate and to defeat their individuality.

Lalu is back, out of prison, with a high hope of getting official favour and the expectation of a grant of land, but he is taken as a liability in the army due to his experience as a German prisoner. For Lalu, this is the first betrayal; he finds his village completely changed:

> ... what was extraordinary, things were not being taken for what they were, as the immutable decree of Fate which no man could alter; why, here were desperate people, forming clubs and bands of the bereft. The water flowing uphill instead of down. (48)

Now there is a voice of protest, a note of dissent, a sound of rebel, a fight for self; there is no question of blind acceptance or surrender. There is a protest meeting and Lalu attends it, and finds himself caught between the two currents and cross-currents, those who favour freedom totally away from the British influence, and the other force which wants honourable compromise with the governing authority; he cannot decide whom he should support. They are interesting characters in the novel: Verma Sahib, a radical professor wedded to theories rather than action; Kanwar Rampal Singh, 'the count' who is a socialist aristocrat, enigmatic and paradoxical, enigmatic because he never makes an important political or social statement and paradoxical because he is part revolutionary and part traditionalist. He is benevolent; before him dispossessed, infuriated by the obsequious deference paid him by his social inferiors and he is genuinely impassioned by the need to rectify some of the glaring inequalities that surround him, yet he is the most satisfying and complex character. Lalu joins the radical group with the count, attends a tea-party given by the Nawab, the most powerful of the landlords who advocates the permanent and irrevocable exploitation of peasants; he speaks at a festival beside the Ganges, advocating riots, until the police fix a demonstration and break up the meeting. The Marxist influence on Anand is visible in the creation of a character like Lalu and the circumstances around him. A young European magistrate who is unpolluted by the ways of the world endorses his innocence on a charge of civil disobedience and Lalu becomes a hero, yet he feels isolated:

> This isolation, he knew, was the price he had to pay for abjuring all connection with the false gods of the world, for seeking to speak and act and live by his faith,by the integrity of his knowledge and of the peasants' lives, by eschewing all thoughts of obedience to the Sarkar which ruled the Indian earth, by becoming an agitator, always on the prowl and in danger of being arrested. (344)

After his return from Europe, Lalu abducts Maya and marries her. Maya is a girl of upper class family and so, at the end of the day, Lalu has to face the music, and the feeling of isolation intensifies. Maya cannot understand his revolutionary instincts or vision and ideology. He feels that by abducting Maya he has defeated that particular class. He is both her ideal and victim; this duality in the relationship remains till the end of the novel. The birth of a child brings hope but still he nourishes the concept of Two Nations, based on the rich and the poor. All these things are dream only and Lalu is again arrested, mistaken for an insurrectionist. With the telegram of the birth of a son, the novel closes, perhaps, with a ray of hope.

This triology is designed to create a character like Lalu, to analyze his motives and to explain his political philosophy. *Untouchable* and *Coolie* are his early novels, somehow analogous to them, revealing an accumulated outrage at the states of India and a profound horror at the apparent petrifaction of the feudal system. Like Bakha and Munoo, Lalu is also born into a state of subservience, but the difference lies in the fact that what Bakha and Munoo passively accept, Lalu forcefully rejects, irrevocably and personally. Lalu becomes a prophet of revolution, a revolution that must be organized and must spring naturally from within the people.

> If the English declare that they won India by the sword and by sword they shall hold it, why can't we say that we shall win India back by the sword and by the sword shall we keep it? (313)

Anand's message in the Lalu triology is the rejection of the extremes of violence and non-violence. It traces the evolution in the person of one betrayed peasant, an Indian everyman and an embodiment of the spirit of India's masses to attain freedom.

Now, let us take Bhabani Bhattacharya whose *Muric for Mohini* is the much acclaimed work and is supposed to be an important Indian English writer. Taken as a whole, this novel presents the theme of synthesis, between village and city, education and superstition, and selflessness and cooperation; it can be traced in plot construction, characterization and view of life, that is, vision. The village offers a sweet bond, because here:

> lived the various caste groups Brahmins, near Brahmins, the professional castes—blacksmith, barbar, washerman milkman—and the largest group of all the peasants, both Hindu and Muslim. (120)

A very good comparison of the city life and the village-life has been presented by the writer, as he says:

> The village had sights and smells and silence denied to hustling cities ... feeling and holding Mother earth with their hands gave them strength and pleasure ...satisfied all senses ...trees heavy with fruit, ponds full of fish ...the space' the clean air to breath, the land covered with greenery, lovely... what have we here in city? Din, dust, hustle, suffocating. (53)

Initially, Mohini dislikes the village life, "City and village are apart. Perhaps they should stay apart: perhaps this inter-marriage is wrong. We girls suffer, not the man."(93)

However, Mohini's anger subsides; her rebel native is softened as the time passes. She gives her approval of her marriage with Jaidev but fails to develop intimacy with the village girls. Harindra, the rebellious social reformer, cannot adjust with the social taboos:

> what folly to try to help such people? why should I waste myself? I am going back to town, Jayadeva. I'll set up a practice in town. (143)

But Jaidev persuades him to stay in the village and educate the ignorant folk. Out of this clash is born the philosophy of compromise. Rooplekha can adjust, though for him, "a city has a little mercy for an alien as the country"(92). She can fit in the life because she is village-bred and city-wed. Mohini is astonished to learn that a city like Calcutta can be cruel, yet she gets integrated in the village life. Rooplekha points out the need of a bridge between the two attitudes of rural and urban, call it compromise or anything else, "The city absorbs a little of the barbaric village, the village absorbs a little of the 'west-polluted' city. Both change, unaware. They are less angry with each other." (94)

This compromise between two modes of life is visible in the marriage of Rooplekha with Calcutta-based surgeon and that of Mohini with a university educated visionary scholar living in a village in preference to leading an academic life in a city. No doubt, the village requires reconstruction and reformation. Harindra has to face antagonism from the village folk in general and from his own family members including his father. There is a fight between the traditional system being practised by his father and the modern system being practised by himself. Kabiraj has to compromise, "The miracle happened. The mother's life was saved. Youths unfurled banner added a proud cubit to its length." (144)

Any village of India suffers from superstition and ignorance which are bound to confront education and enlightenment. The mother stands for all superstitions, prejudices and taboos, but she has to bow down finally: "Old mother had compromised with modernity and her struggle to uphold the orthodox way was without passion. But the mother of the Big House was stern, the old and of the new; this mother hadnothing in her native that would allow change." (130)

The couple, Jaidev and Mohini, has to fight a lot against superstition and ignorance in order to educate the illiterate villages, to equip them with adequate knowledge. Mohini runs a school to serve the purpose, as an eager teacher and ardent lover. Thus the synthesis is with the characterization also. With the reconciliation between Jaidev and his mother life for Mohini becomes sweet and harmonious, like a music throbbing with every pulsation of her innermost being, as it would be like for New India with the regeneration of social set-up under the influence of modernization. This novel depicts clash and compromise in a decent way. It also projects the integration of a variety of philosophical and conceptual integration. The novelist talks of other freedom except the political freedom. Jaidev puts it as such, " India was on the verge of freedom: a new page of world history was writing itself. The political implications were visible to all but not the social problems. What was political liberty worth to the common man if it was not part of renascence in social life." (67)

He also elaborates his feeling to Mohini when he says, "our political freedom is worth little without social uplift" (127). Jaidev is Gandhian prototype and his progressive mind invites qualities from every corner of the world, which can be better known as harmony of culture. Jaidev symbolizes the amalgamation of the past and the present, the old and the new, the traditional and the modern, the village and the city, horoscope and microscope. He tells his wife:

> Thought had to be related to action. Abstraction had to be resolved in human terms. The philosopher had to step out of his temple of silence and lead his people across the valley of conflict and discord to end social slaveries. (138)

This novel can be cited as the meeting point of thought with action, of contemplation with commitment, of asceticsm with aestheticism on and so on and so forth. Such an integration is not available in any of the Indian English writing of Diaspora writers and it makes it exclusive and extraordinary.

Another important Indian English writer is Rabindranath Tagore who is responsible to bring about Renaissance in this sphere. His imprint of a genius can be traced in his short stories also which are known for the combination of lyricism with realism. We can easily locate rich emotionalism with the realism of the poor, and the middle class of villages and small towns. His short stories are related to the affairs of the common folk, their hopes and aspirations, disappointments and frustrations, joys and sorrows in human life. He is basically a Bengali writer and his work was later on translated in English.

His story 'The Postmaster' is about human psychology dealing with indescribable grief of a village orphan girl Ratan working in the postmaster's house, doing odd domestic jobs. When the postmaster has an attack of malaria, she works as a nurse day and night. Now the postmaster has resigned fom his post and prepares to leave for Calcutta. Ratan wants to accompany him but he refuses. Instead, he gives her some money which she refuses. Ratan wants love but she is shocked and dazed at the inhuman behaviour of the postmaster who finally departs caring least about Ratan. Tagore has made a psychological study of the mind of an orphan girl, who is nothing, but victim of circumstances. In 'The Castaway', Tagore studies the mind of an adolescence. In yet another story 'The Kabuliwalla' the aggressive character of Kabuliwalla is shown breaking the superstition. Rahmat, a heavy, awkward, unlettered and uncouth person from Afghanistan sells nuts, dry fruits and lends money at interest. Mini is a Bengali five-year-old girl with whom he comes in contact and becomes friendly taking her as his own daughter. But Mini takes him as a notorious man who may take her away in a big bag, yet she accepts all his gifts. All of a sudden, the story takes a turn and he is jailed for eight years for stabbing a man who refused to return his money. He comes out of prison and finds Mini turned into a beautiful lady and getting married. He gives her nuts and dry fruits and returns back to his homeland to meet his own daughter whose imprint of hand he always carried. Here Tagore tries to establish the nature of love and affection which bear no barrier of race, religion, age, education and social prejudice; it is also a study of the parental love which is always everywhere the same.

Another noteworthy story is 'The Hungry Stories' which creates a mood of half-pity and half-awe. The story moves around the life and death of Kusum; the super-natural relationship among Kusum, the sanyasi, the river, the ghat and the hungry stories is also projected here. It blends supernaturalism with realism, but the supernatural does not transgress the realism. A solitary palace of the Mughal emperor Mahmud II forms the background of the story but the heartaches and blasted hopes transmitted throughout these years still persist in every thirsty and hungry stone of the place eager to devour any living being who chances to come near it.

'The Home-coming' is a study of the adolescent mind of a village lad of 14 years who goes to his uncle's home in Calcutta. It portrays a mischievous boy's pathetic predicament caused by his transplantation from his native rural home into the oppressive atmosphere of his uncle's home.

'The Child's Return', is an interesting psychological study of a simple but loyal servant who is overwhelmed as it were by a sudden tragic experience. The servant's mind is revealed: he is superstitious and half-idiotic and fails to adjust himself to a tragic situation. Tagore is a stern realist who grapples with the hard problems of contemporary life, a realistic appraisal of the social content and a brutally frank approach to the psychological complexities of human life.

Precisely the approach of Tagore is entirely different from the Indian English writers of Diaspora. The analysis of the works of the above-said writers confirms the fact that the writings of Indian English writers are different in the construction of plot, characterization and approach or technique of presentation.

Works Cited

Anand, M. R., *The Village,* Bombay: Kutub, 1954.

_______ *Across the Black Water*, London: Jonathan Cape, 1940.

_______ *The Sword and the Sickle*, London: Jonathan Cape, 1942.

Bhttcharya, Bhabani, *Music for Mohini,* New Delhi, Orient, 1952.

Iyenger, K.R.S., *Indian Writing in English*, New Delhi: Sterling Pub., 1994.

Narayan, R.K., *The Guide,* Mysore: Indian Thought, 1972.

Rao, Raja, *The Serpent and the Rope*, New Delhi: Orient,1968.

_______ *The Cat and Shakespeare,* New Delhi: Orient, 1971.

6

Convulsion as Acceptance

Indian English Diaspora writing brought a sort of convulsion in the lot of Indian English writing and the global writing as a whole, sharing some common ingredients and feelings of any other Diaspora writing with certain inalienable characteristics of its own. They merged in the mainstream to make it an organic whole for the existing resonance and future generation, taking as acceptance to the main corpus of literature. For a proper understanding of Diasporic cultural and literary engagements across geographies, histories, nations and communities we need a thorough penetration in the subtle nuances of the complex terrain of Diasporic experience, and its different dimensions. Manjit Inder Singh in the 'Introduction' of his book *Contemporary Diasporic Literature* writes:

> ... debates over theoretical, cultural and historical resonances of the term have proliferated in the academy about problematications of Diaspora and nation. And, arguably the explosion in various fields—literature, sociology anthropology, film studies, queen theory area and ethnic studies makes it somewhat confusing about its blurring into boundaries and margins, how diaspora is being deployed in critical scholarship. For all its privileged history and complex connotations, diaspora is a buzzword, a catch-all phrase to represent or speak for all movements, theorizations of hybridity and cross-cultural, multi-ethnic dislocations. (10)

Diaspora begins with homelessness, belongingness and identity. It takes its root with 'exile' and finally finds refuge in some alien climate. It also points out to the problem of locations and dislocations, placement and displacement, habitation and inhabitation. Memory and nostalgia are the two terms that help the Diaspora individuals in regaining a ground of meaning to a great extent. Bender crossing and relocations bring the concept of hybridity and syncretism. However, the actual living experiences of human beings located in specific geographical locations acquaint us with the actual status of Diaspora, as that of exiles in a battle of Waterloo; its anguish and intensity never be rationalized. In fact, the term 'location' or 'dislocation' simply denotes the existential state. Lukas regards the novel as an expression of transcendental homelessness; Dante, Canard and many others dwell on the same state; yet now is the time when homelessness and dislocation have acquired a vast scale of magnitude. Gurubhagat Singh defines it as follows:

> Expatriate writing, in its theory and practice, is the work of the exile that has experienced unsettlement at the existential, political and metaphysical levels. With this experience, he/she has unsettled the philosophical and aesthetic systems. The phenomenon of exile has emerged in our times due to uneven development within capitalism, and due to the movement forced by colonial powers. (21)

This uneven development is responsible for huge migration of Asians and Africans to the West. Such immigrant individuals mentally work with two epistemologies. No doubt, after losing the centre that used to unify they have dismantled their intermingled visions, and hybridity becomes an existential truth. It affects the theory and foundation, determining specific aesthetics which is two-dimensional: one, the external colonial or modernist and the second the internal or national; it shapes the personal identity; the Diasporic self has to undergo a trial during which it deals with these centres, sometimes rejecting and sometimes accepting them. Raja Rao is very optimistic when he says, "I carry India with me whenever I go." Yet Uma Parmeswaran feels:

> ... when one arrives in a new land, one has a sense of wonder and adventure at the sight and feel of a landscape so different from what one has been accustomed to; there is also a sense of isolation and fear; and intense nostalgia

> is a buffer to which many retreat. The different voices in my *Trishanku* express these different emotions in different ways. (32)

Nostalgia is the most striking feature of Diaspora and the characters have a romanticized view of their native land until it paralyzes them completely as a toxic does to the addict. It happened with V.S. Naipaul and so came the works like *An Area of Darkness* and *India: A Wounded Civilization* which misrepresent India and nothing else. Uma Parmeswaran is optimistic of the fair gender which can accommodate the two homes at a time—without conflict or ambivalence. Other striking features of Diaspora writings are that of dissemination and alienation as an integral part of experience of expatriation and transplantation. Ashis Gupta questions:

> Is it desperation, greed, rootlessness, or a loss of idealism that is driving Indians—often a country's most valuable resources away from their homelands? Cultural change, and the cross fertilization of cultures, appears unstoppable in this day and age, except by dictatorial decree ... sociologist tells us that every new social construct contains the germs of the past. (48)

P.A. Abraham quotes Aritha Van Hank in his article 'Crisis of Unbelonging' as the challenge of expatriate reading and writing:

> Imagine a country as this country is, peopled by characters who have abandoned their setting and who seek to plot their own story in a new way. They choose to displace themselves to surrender the familiar ... curiously enough, because they make the choices, they are happy, if not always satisfied with their story, and the effects of displacement only begin to appear in the children a grandchildren. Some people would say that it is only a matter of adapting to a new environment, or adjusting to a custom, of learning a language. I maintain that it is much more profound, a displacement so far—reaching that it only vanishes after several generations I learned that the world was fiction and fiction was refuge. (50)

In the post-colonial literature the term 'expatriate' is considered to be legitimate which has a hidden impulse of literary journey towards have, history, memory and past. They have to face rejection at every step and so they have to cling to ethnic identity which is, at times, considered to be derogatory. They are caught between two worlds and two cultures, and so they have to go for a new space and have to face the problem of language also. Consequently anxieties for home and homelessness become the perennial theme of the writings of this community.

According to George Steiner the expatriate writer is 'contemporary everyman' with a longing for the past, pain for exile and homelessness, double vision of looking forward and a yearning backward. P.A. Abraham opines, "No matter where you lived, even if you lived in the same place all your life, you would look at the past, at lost moments at lost opportunities, lost loves." (51)

Bharati Mukherjee emigrated to Canada, married a Canadian writer, Clark Blaise, and is now residing in America, so she is an Indian expatriate. She admits that writing is a political act for her. She suffers from a personal sense of marginalization of women and her stories speak for it. As a writer she was invisible and as a woman of colour she was visible in the Canadian society; this is a paradoxical state of affairs, as she observes:

> I was a psychological expatriate, though a naturalized Canadian for fifteen years, simply because Canada is a country officially hostile to the concept of assimilation. It proclaims the virtue of its multicultural policy. Perceiving myself to be in a comfortable unwelcoming environment. I struggled to maintain various emblems of my difference. (57)

This expatriation makes the writer restrictive and self-defeating; always in a mood of complaint, projecting the pain of exile and becoming a figure of solitude. She has faced hostility and we can notice her personal trauma in her statement:

> ...the attitude of in the sixties and seventies was that if one hadn't played in snow and grown up eating oatmeal

> one didn't have anything relevant to say to Canadian readers. The seventies were horrendous for Indians in Canada. There was a lot of bigotry against Canadian citizens of Indian origin, especially in Toronto... . Toronto made me a civil right activist I wrote about the devastating personal effects of racism. (58)

In the early novels of Bharati Mukherjee, such as, *The Tiger's Daughter* (1971) and *Wife* (1975) the major theme is that of expatriation used as a compulsion, condition and metaphor for deeper level of solitude and alienation because expatriation is both geographically and mentally making the protagonists Tara and Dimple uncomfortable in both native and alien cultures. They have to face the recognition of duality of fluid identity. In her collection of stories *Darkness* (1985) Bharati writes in the 'Introduction', that she saw her Indianness not "as a fragile identity to be preserved against obliteration ... but as a set of fluid identities to be celebrated"(3); it is a collection of uneasy stories about Indian expatriation.

No doubt, there is no universal standard of expatriate writing and it is good for its health because universal standards dehistoricize and depoliticize literary texts and make it a narrow self serving the parochialism of Europe. And when there is the problem of cultural differences no universal criteria can be worked out. A writer's individual talent is rooted in the tradition of a particular society and culture. Modern literary imagination has its strength in evocation of the individual's predicament which further defined in alienation, immigration, expatriation, exile and quest for identity. In the alien land, the individual may feel estranged culturally and linguistically but his social, emotional, ethnic, or cultural identity assumes mythic proportions and becomes an unattainable ideal. To identity difference within a culture is different from categorization because the difference serves to invigorate a culture, and preserves a static distribution of social power to keep it alive, which can be known as egalitarian and hierarchical. The egalitarian opens opportunities for change and the hierarchial operates as a catalyst for keeping cultures apart in the name of tradition.

Such identity dilemma finds its articulation in Diaspora writings. In the absence of a centre, locus or home, it becomes a problem, and involves images of journeys and displacements to alternative homes: in either cases, leaving a home and arriving at a new home. The settlers have to interact with other social relations determined by class, race, ethnicity, racism, gender and sexuality. All these factors go in the making of a configuration of Diaspora literature. In the process of identity formation the heterogeneity of the Diaspora constitutes the soul as it transcend transnational and trans-cultural boundaries. Obviously when a home becomes a mythic space of desire it also assumes a place of no real return. Thus the term 'home' gets different connotations: the actual geographical space of origin refigured and reinvented through imagination, and the lived experience of present-day reality with local sounds, smells and sights. This paradoxical situation brings confliction and tension in Diaspora literature, and the writer's identity shapes the text in crucial ways, depending on the concrete and tangible everyday realities, such as, one's allegiance to a nation, culture and family, especially ones emotional rooting.

Evidently, the Diasporic writer is located in the multicultural contexts drawing its impulses from the interconnections between the unique specificity of a life and a sense of belongingness to the community at large that falls in elusive, descriptive and analytical category. The term, Diaspora, has inherent diversities and yet it attempts to homogenize, though it is not possible to encapsulate the dynamic energies that seethe therein. Diasporic movements are located at the heart of cultural encounters and often crucial historical junctures which, as variables, are in a status of continuous revision and flux. Diaspora is a complex term, and it is essential to understand its varied ramifications and examine its inadequacies to get a proper definition. What brings unity to the scattered community is the sense of common homeland and the experience of displacement. In *India—A Million Mutinies Now,* V.S. Naipaul talks of Diasporic communities. Cut off from India by a distance they developed something they would never have known in India, a sense of belonging to an Indian community. Despite enormous diversities, there are no homogeneous or monolithic notions of home or identity, and we find a swing between nostalgia and anguish, anger/cynicism and love, reconciliation and acceptance. Consequently, the themes are often social and political concerns, and the contradictions that the writer perceives mirrored in the contemporary fabric are perhaps a reflection or his a her own contradictory psychic pulls, the uncertainties, etc. Obviously, the writer's sensibility is shaped by the act of leaving and settling elsewhere, and it also shapes the text, so the epistemology of home matters a lot. In the case of political and other exiles a sense of impassioned indignation or outrage comes up, and the text becomes literature of resistance. The Diasporic writers often write of perennial outsider status and the subsequent alienation awarding a fluid space wherein memory can intervene to create unreal and often distorted images. In the case of Salman Rushdie his peculiar positionality becomes a determinant of his thematic preoccupations; the self-reflexivity of metafiction is the result of his inability to look at home and look away from it. This sense of estrangement touches the notion of home, the land and places of our birth which remain in our memory as a dream and as nostalgia, with a sense of belongings.

Truly speaking Diaspora literature is about sensibility rather than space where nothing in particular can be traced. What dominates the thematic pegs are the issues of identity, home, dislocations, relocations, rootlessness and belonging whereas multicultural contexts provide settings. On the other hand, Diaspora is also taken to be an ever developing concept, and it cannot be generalized, homogenized and universalized. It is neither static nor closed, and is never fit for final analysis or examination. Yet we get several questions that puzzle us; for instance:

a) How does cultural value get encoded through myth and gender stereotype?

b) Does the role of the writer and the dilemma of gender?

c) Are the subversive strategies used by the writer for re-inventing identity indicative of her location in the real world as well as the inability to speak in other ways?

d) Are all acts of reading, re-thinking and re-inventing conventional children's stories, fairy tales, myths, etc. acts of explanations and reconfigurations?

Namjoshi answers the question of identity taking it as a philosophical and real term in *Because of India*:

> It's apparent that the components of core identity change from place to place and period to period. Today the main components seemed to be based on gender, skin colour, and sexual choice, as well as other factors such as nationality and religions, which are more or less important in different places. Any threat to the sense of self causes a violent reaction. (83-84)

Truly speaking, home is a metaphorical and conceptual space, wherever it may be physically situated, and for the Diasporic person as a writer it is continually configured in huge diverse and affirmative ways. We cannot generalize or homogenize the contemporary floating/moving populations, and the concepts of home, homecoming, identity, alienation, loss, forgetting, memory, rootlessness are global issues with ever-changing configurations. We may quote Hugh of St. Victa, a twelfth century mystic, who says:

> The man who finds his homeland sweet is still a tender beginner; he to whom every soil is as his native one is already strong; but he is perfect to whom the entire world is as a foreign land. The tender soul has fixed his love on one spot in the world; the strong man has extended his love to all places; the perfect man has extinguished his.

It is relevant to quote Salman Rushdie who privileges the migrant writer on the ground that he can see both from inside and outside which the indigenous writer cannot. He says so in *A Dangerous Art Form* (4). In the location of culture, Homi Bhabha talks of culture as a strategy of survival (172). In *Outside in the Teaching Machine* Gayatri Spivak asks the indigenous elite or the metropolitans marginal not to produce a merely antiquarian history which seeks the continuities of soil, language and urban life in which resent is rooted (64). In *In Theory* Aijaz Ahmed favours cultural nationalism calling it the constitutional ideology of the theoretical positions from which there issues are raised (67). Viney Kripal in her 'Introduction' to *The Post-Modern Indian English Novel* says:

> *Brennan in Salman Rushdie and the Third World'* demolishes persuasively the claims that the cosmopolitan writer empowers the diasporic communities when he or she writes from the interstitial perspective of the contingently acquired hybridity. (3)

In fact, Diaspora experience is as varied as it can be because the Diaspora community has migrated due to various reasons which may be economic, social, political or for trade and commerce, as religious preachers, as labourers, convicts or soldiers, as expatriates or refugees, exiles (forced or voluntary) or as guest workers in search of a better life and opportunities—but all of them share common experiences; their commonalities as well as the differences are based on their conditions of migrations and period of stag in the adopted land. Home is the first trauma of all migrants; the reminiscences of their motherland and the anguish of leaving behind that "they continue to relate personally or vicariously, to the homeland in a way or another and their ethno-communal consciousness and solidarity are importantly defined by the existence of such a relationship." (Safran,1991)

There migrants aspire for a home and more importantly wish to go back to their own home. Safran opines, "Diaspora consciousness is an intellectualization of an existential condition, a sad condition that is ameliorated by an imaginary homeland to which one hopes one will some day return." (Safran, 1991)

Dislocation and unsettlement are the experiences common to all in the alien land. Dislocation brings breakage from the old identity and the unacceptance of the host society brings in alienation. The immigrants form the marginal group which tries to assimilate, adopt and integrate with the host society, simultaneously trying to preserve their original culture and identity. This is a step towards insulation from the dominant host group and the tool that is used is the continuance of the cultural practices and said customs, along with their religion, language, music, art, dress, cuisine, etc. It continues from generation to generation. In the process some disappear and some syncretise or change. Meanwhile, they develop a double identity, a status of Trishanker, neither to the maternal place nor to their foster country, and their culture becomes a sandwich culture. The feelings of rootlessness, alienation, confusion, nostalgia, dislocation, and suffering due to discrimination based on race, culture, religion and language culminate into conflicts, fight for identity, all leading to the creation of a fractured psyche.

The immigrant is always caught between the two worlds, and he has to negotiate with a new space; similarly he is caught between cultures and languages. The Diasporic writer also negotiates with a new literary space; the splintered psyche sheds off its new neurosis, he is compelled to write and write back. With his multicultural ethos and a deep understanding of socio-cultural and economic realities around he is successful in transmuting his experience into writing. Such writing helps him forge a cultural identity. These writings illustrate their own awareness of their history and heritage, society and its problems, along with achievements, limitations and frustrations. A Diasporic text can be analyzed in terms of location, dislocation and relocation. It talks of sweat and toil often washed with tears of achievement despite impediments of education, advancements and progress. It is about traumas, anguishes and challenges, and finally about open spaces and not about closed spaces. It is about intermingling and interruptions, as the joy of double vision and pain of being split, as a different history, distant culture and fluid memory. It has developed its own theoretical position privileging double vision and as a part of post-colonialism.

The immigrants employ three different techniques of adaptation of Indians abroad. They are assimilation, cultural preservation with economic integration and ethnic polarization for pursuit of power cultivations. The most profound and predominant pattern is the cultural preservation with economic integration. It results in the development of double identity, sandwich culture, plural society of sojourners.

'Insulator and Aperture' is the name of the model on the basis of which the concept of sandwich culture is developed which comprises the conviction that the outsiders become insiders to merge their identity and gain a certain degree of acceptance by host society. Some such apertures are intermarriage, adopting names of the host society, adoption of the language of the host society, promotion of inter-commensality, adoption of food habits and developing a taste for host cuisine. On the other hand, insulatory mechanisms are retention of mother tongue, provision of separate educational facilities for children by opening schools in the host country, formation of voluntary organizations, pursuit of parental religion, continuation of food habits and taboos associated with eating, retention of manner of dressing, particularly that of women folk, keeping aperture open for the parent culture, using the text books and reading material in separates schools, exposure to mediabooks, music, films, videos, postal and telecommunications. There is a possibility of poly-ethnic relations in such societies. Cultural manifestations are taken as the product of changing political circumstances in the Diasporic locations seen as cultural responses to such situations.

Taking into view the entire gamut of Indian English writing, it can be noticed that the major Indian writers in English write from Diaspora spaces in the West, as if the centre of gravity of Indian English writing has shifted abroad and so representation of Indianness become contentious. Writers like Naipaul, Vassanji, Bissoondath, Satendra Nandan, Peter Nazareth, Cyril Davydeen, David Dabydeen, Jhumpa Lahiri, Bidisha Bandopadhyay, Mura Syal, Shani Mootoo, Shauna Singh Baldwin, Chitra Divakaruni, etc. refuse to be called Indian, though they have their origins in India, in some cases removed by two or three generations. Yet the study of Diasporic discourse is a new emerging field of interest.

Indian Diaspora communities have rarely been engendered by war, privation, psychic or physical brutalities. Poverty has been one of the prominent reasons for them to leave the home, so they are not disinherited lot. The paradigms of Diaspora discourse kept pace with the changing cultural situation as a result of cultural interface, sharpening its perception and definition of the myriad different compositions of identity in these situations. If we go by the history of Diaspora studies, which is also known as Transnational Studies, we come to know that identity and belongingness are essentially processes in change mediated by issues of ethnicity, gender and sexuality. In fact, Diaspora theory is essentially a discourse about the 'other', about the 'difference. The issue of migration and its effect on the Diaspora subjectivities is central to it. There is a variety of Diaspora situations depending upon the kinds of migrations because the effect of migration is contingent upon the relationship of the Diaspora space with the host country and the ethnic difference. So many conditioning factors operate and the theory resists homogenization of ethnicity. The most often made assumptions of Diaspora discourse is dislocation and homelessness but in the changing situation individuals in multicultural contexts have reversed these assumptions in multicultural contexts where dislocation and homelessness turn out to be mere theoretical constructs. We have writers with multiple homes involving multiple migrations, such as, Vassanji, Peter Nazareth and Shani Mootoo; or these writers, India is the home of their ancestors and it is only an abstraction. We have writers like Meera Syal, Hari Kunzru, Kiran Desai, Jhumpa Lahiri, Shauna Singh Baldwin and Mira Kamdar who had their upbringing abroad and in India they find themselves out of place; only due to their Indian origian they are bracketed under Indian Diaspora. With the opening of boundaries, the Diaspora self is changing in character raising myriad complex questions about construction of identity, history and nation. Mongrelization and homogeneity are seen to define the contemporary condition, especially of the succeeding generations of immigrant parents.

To talk of Diaspora means talking of the sandwiched; it is the day of in-betweenness. Such novice tendencies challenge the old assumptions, and the immigrant generation can no longer be regarded as displaced communities because in most places they are a sizeable community of affluence and influence, and enjoy a greater sense of community than their home country. The transnational technologies also help in stabilising the linkages. The post-colonial tendency to preserve the local identity has resulted in the Indian Diaspora becoming increasingly assertive in its ethnicity in such mutricultural contexts, and practise aggressive and ostentatious Indian rituals of birth, marriage, festivals, etc. to the points of self-exotification. It also manifest the sense of insecurity and expression of strength and solidarity. Such attempts justify the construction of temples for worship, establishment of Indian grocery stores, setting up of exclusive desi news groups, online journals and self-help groups, making of their own crossover films, etc. Now the problems of dislocation and identity have diluted to a great extent, and global organizations have emerged to promote the ethnic identities and cultures and writing of India and Indians Diaspora in transnational context. That is why we have writers like Hari Kunzru, Shauna Singh Baldwin, Jhumpa Lohiri, Mira Kamdar, Bidira Bandopadhyag, Mura Syal, etc. who celebrate their hybridity and ethnicity in the countries of adoption and some of them even disown their Indian connection. Obviously in such a context, the words 'Diaspora' or 'expatriate' with all their linguistic and historical connotations, accretions and associations would fail to describe their factual condition. Yet the semantics and semiotics of identity, difference, belonging, memory and desire are much more complex in the Diaspora discourse than could be indicated in nomenclature. The frame of Diaspora is provided by migration, dislocation and cultural difference, and its consequences reflected in the lived experience of individuals and groups at ground zero in myriad forms. Writers define identity and hybridity in several ways, and they unequivocally celebrate their heterogeneity in the open societies and multicultural contexts. They feel free to dispute the politics of hyphen and seek alliance with the mainstream politics to seize power. They live in the interstices in the host countries, and their perception of identity is mediated by issues of their class, ethnicity, gender and sexuality. In the Diaspora situation, there is a shift in the cultural plurality to make space for the 'other' out of intellectual enquiry, which finally proves that polyculturalism is an irreversible fact today and a way of life.

Writers of Indian Diaspora—we may call them writers of Indian origin—celebrate their ethnicity and are encouraged to write ethnocentric books which have a negative impact, being accused of 'musems of exoticism', 'native informants', etc., with questions of authenticity of Indian images. Out of such convulsion, come up the Diasporic theory with the multiplicies of their situations, and gradually evolve into a discourse of opposition to a discourse of dialogue. Such discourses go beyond theoretical constructs and adopt themselves to the ever-changing lived reality of cultural dynamics in the Diaspora experience. The theoretical generalization come from the ways identities are practical, lived and experienced. Sukalpa Bhattacharjee has explored its status in the postcolonial world in her book, *Postcolonial Literature: Essays on Gender, Theory and Genres:*

> The uprooting of postcolonial populations has generated a vocabulary of migrancy and has also raised questions about the role of postcolonial intellectuals in the constructions of diasporic consciousness. Narratives of migrancy and diaspora have always provided for a productive silts for postcolonial resistance with the dislocation of postcolonial intellectuals in the metropolis. That is how the metropolitan discourse have framed contemporary conceptions of hybridity and migrancy... The postcolonial and post-modern theorization of power and identity have not adequately addressed the nexus of historical, political, economic, cultural and ideological forces affecting the constructions and consumptions of postcolonial realities and representations which involve border crossing of the postcolonial and the postmodern. (101)

The status of Diaspora is also called the state of learning 'in between' which includes the marginalized indigenous people, the subalterns, indigenous and aboriginal women, refuges, internees, and immigrant writers, and the narratives of migrancy and Diaspora substantiate the conceptualization of the in-between. This is what S. Bhattacharya feels. She explores altogether different diamension when she says:

> ... such narratives question the essentialist models and ideology of a unified natural/cultural norm, one that underpins the centre/margin model of colonialist discourse. They also question the simple kinds of theories of nativism which suggest that decolonization can be affected by a recovery or reconstruction of pre-colonial societies. (102)

Most surprisingly, the Diasporic identity has been adopted by many writers as a positive affirmation of their hybridity, and we should also notice that migrancy, Diaspora, and exile have become politically changed words, though it is more related to the pain of loss of self and the paradox of identity construction of migrant and Diasporic cultures in their status of place/non-place, border/non border, presence/non-presence, and the dilemmas like that. However, it should be noted that the Diaspora individual is free in his physical and mental movements beyond the shackles of national history and politrics. In fact, the development of migrant sensibility is one of the central themes of this century and it is directly related to displaced persons, which construct its own contingent truths, makes a singular repository of experience and resistance, critical archival material of alternative covens and its own paradigms.

Edward Said is more relevant in this concern. In his essay titled, "Third World Intellectuals and Metropolitan Culture", he terms the Diaspora figure as the most authentic embodiment of the post-colonial intellectual. In his essay, "Identity, Authority and Freedom" he says that "our model of academic freedom should be the migrant of traveler." Salman Rushdie observes in *Imaginary Homeland:*

> The effect of mass migration has been the creation of radically new types of human being: people who root themselves in ideas rather than places, in memories as much as in material things; people who have been obliged to define themselves—because they are so defined by others—by their otherness; people in whose depart selves strange fusions occur and where they find themselves. (124)

After large-scale decolonization, particularly in the 1960, the world could witness a massive uprooting; no doubt, the reason was economic and political. The New World order has created a sense of multiple belonging, and so the meaning of identity, location and culture has become more complex and margins have become more important in the neo-colonial global capitalism. It is the target of attack—to be destroyed, replaced, expanded and incorporated as new territorial acquisition, as novel fields of inquiry of the fractured subject.

This fractured migrant imagination is an imperializing consciousness imposing itself upon the world (103). She also points out two variations in migrancy:

> one involves an existential condition of homelessness with a concomitant attitude of autonomy and detachment as the privileged locus of imaginative experience the other validates multiplicity and hybridity of subject positions generating a feeling of belonging to several even too many homes. (103)

Major icons of modernism like Conard, Joyce, James, Pound and Eliot embody and represent exile as a painful yet exquisitely enabling experience for the artistic consciousness.

However, the recent study of Diaspora delinks distress from dislocation and adheres to the idea of belonging everywhere by belonging nowhere. Salman Rushdie in his book *Satanic Verses* offers the perspective of the two post-colonial identities: one is that of the migrant and the other is national, and says that 'exile is a soulless country.' (208)

Nailpaul can be cited as an external exile and Rushdie as permanent migrancy. Multiple dislocation opens up abundance of alternative locations, allowing the individual to own several homes which culminates in deterritorialized consciousness away from the collective entiry of race, class, gender, or nation. Rushdie says:

> Indian writers in England include political exiles, first generation migrants, affluent expatriates whose residence here is frequently temporary, naturalized Britans, and people born here who may never have laid eyes on the subcontinent ... Indian writers in England have accent to a second tradition, quite apart tradition, quite apart from their racial history. It is the culture and political history

> of the phenomenon of migration, displacement, life in a minority group. ... Huguenots the Irish, the Jews: the past to which one belongs is an English part, the history of immigrant Britain. Swift, Conand, Marx are as much the literary forbears as Tagore and Raja Ram Mohan Roy. (17-20)

The complex category of migrant writers remains unrepresented in post-colonial and post-modern studies and hence has been located in the in-between space; the formation of this category is known as ethno-racial formation. Distance from home is a major stimulus to a creative writer because exile creates a kind of isolation which is nearer to freedom. The concept of a single home or belongingness is meaningless today. Now is the time of multiple home, multiple identity and multiple belonging. So a migrant has to float up word from history and his journey across the histories and cultures of the world transforms the myth of his ontological unbelonging to a larger myth of excess of belonging. This dialectic of belonging and unbelonging constitutes one of the social conditions of the Third World subject into a subject of the in-between. Such writings have an urge to break down all stable semiology, and represent a more autonomous articulation, and the worst thing that it has, what Rushdie calls, 'the emptiness of one's luggage'. The descendants have developed their own culture which is distinctive, and have preservation of their original cultures. It modifies indigenous cultures as a creolized version of their practices, and thus Diaspora, dispersion and dissemination acquire a new significance. Jasbir Jain in her article, "The New Parochialism: Homeland in the Writing of the Indian Diaspora" says:

> The claims of diaspora writing in terms of critical attention theoretical formulations and relationships to cultures of origin and adoption are many. These claims may at times be contradictory, representing momentary adjustments and impulses and draw attention to the complex nature of diaspora existence and writing. (79)

The biggest question that is raised by the Diaspora writing is about home and identity, and when we talk of identity, it is national identity. Salman Rushdie says:

> A full migrant suffers, traditionally, a triple disruption: he loss his place, he inters into an alien language' and he finds himself surrounded by beings whose social behaviour and code is very unlike, and sometimes even offensive to his own. And this is what makes migrants such important figures: because roots, language and social norms have been three of the most important parts of the definition of what it is to be human being. The migrant, denied all three, is obliged to find new ways of describing himself, new ways of being human. But I want to go further than such literalistic discussions; because migration also offers us one of the richest metaphors of our age. The very word metaphor with its roots in Greek words of bearing across, described a sort of migration, the migration of ideas into images. Migrants- borne-across humans-are metaphorical beings in their very essence, and migration, seen as a metaphor, is everywhere around us. We all cross frontiers; that sense, we are all migrant peoples. (Gunter Gross: *On Writing and Politics*, IX-X)

Besides being a question/dilemma of identity, home, culture and belongingness, the Diaspora writing deals with the question of the 'other'. Binda Bose in his article 'Footnoting History: The Disaporic Imagination of Amitav Ghose', writes:

> ... we have been always concerned with the 'other'. It is no doubt fitting that in the age of an extravagant embracing of globalization, we may claim to have closed the gap between battling the 'other' and straddling 'It' certainly, the legacy of postcolonial angst today appears to have settled into a potentially numbering acceptance of bio- or multicultural euphoria (235).

The Diaspora writers themselves define the loss of their writing and, definitely, they examine, rather critically examine, their own literature and their own being. To quote Salman Rushdie:

> Exiles or emigrants or expatriates are haunted. by same sense of loss, same urge to reclaim, to took back, even at the risk of being mutated into pillars of salt. But if we do look back, we must also do so in the knowledge-which given rise to profound uncertainties—that our physical alienation from India almost inevitably means that we will not be capable of reclaiming precisely the thing that was

> lost; that we will, in short, create fictions, not actual cities or villages, but invisible ones, imaginary homelands, India's of the mind. (76)

No doubt, Indian Diaspora is the term that was first used largely in the context of the Jewish experience outside the Jewish homeland, and now it is being used in the contexts of a variety of transnational ethnic experiences. It offers a new paradigm to study Indian cultural productions outside the Indian centre such as Fiji, Singapore, Trinidad, USA, France, Canada, etc., that too, merely in national or regional contexts. Such Diaspora paradigms enable a global approach and initiate a new perspective. It also leads us to the unresolved tensions in the Diasporic consciousness shaping the texts and the ethnohistorical significance of the texts.

We may examine a few Diaspora writers to vindicate our stand, for instance, the most popular being V.S. Nailpaul, a towering figure among the contemporary Diaspora writers, whose chief philosophical concern is the betrayals of history, giving voice to the many ambivalences of the post-colonial Diasporic Indian consciousness. In his text we find his despair, obsessive preoccupations with exile, rootlessness, alienation, and less criticism of newly independent societies. His vision of history condemns post-colonial failures and passes devastating judgment upon the dreams and deeds of the colonizer. It mocks all human endeavour whether weak or strong probably shaped by his Hindu consciousness; yet despite his ambivalence toward his ancestral homeland, despite his occasional rejection of it, India continues to claim her prodigal child unequivocally. This Hindu root is also viewed in *The Serpent and the Rope* which can be termed as quasi-autobiographical testimony created in order to heal his physical exile from India through spiritual reconnection with the geographical home.

India, in most of the Diasporic fiction, is more than a geographical space; it is a region of the mind. As a result all characters of his work perform a journey which finally end in India. Rootlessness is primary in his work and it is a kind of autobiographical ingredient that comes from the rootlessness of his personal life, as Lynda Prescott makes it clear:

> His personal sense of rootlessness, derived from the experience of growing up in an immigrant community in Trinidad and then living as a rather restless exile in England, gives a sharp edge to his emphasis on the social necessity of history. In practically all his work he affirms, directly or indirectly, the need for individuals and whole societies to know and to understand their history in order to make sense of the present. (550)

Salman Rushdie, on the other hand, employs the narrative modes which reveal a philosophical outlook shaped by the contradictions of his own immigrant experience, reconstructing the history of the subcontinent. Not only that, he has a different view of the world and he indulges in fiction with a different purpose:

> ...the world beyond the looking glass, where nonsense is the only sense (Pen Against the Sword, 57) ... the acceptance that all that is solid has melted into air, that reality and morality are constructs, is the point from which fiction begins. (*Is Nothing Sacred*, 9)

His characters travel the irrational depths of human personality whose dreams and nightmares are illogical and nonsensical. We can cite the instance of the cult master of Chupland of *Harmoun and the Sea and Other Stories,* who is observed with the idea of controlling the world; he is poisoning the ocean of stories and is having a plug assembled to stem the very source from which stories spring. In *Midnight's Children* Ahmed Sinai dreams of dictating curses and sorcery to kill dogs; in *Shame* Sufiya has things locked up in her head; in *The Satanic Verses* Farishta wrestles with the voices he hears and the vision he sees. All these characters are created in absurd situations with absurd conceptions, and Rushdie interweaves the subjective with the objective and the personal with the universal, and finally becomes incomprehensible.

Rushdie offers a more apt inquiry into the predicament of modern man as an immigrant writer who is displaced, dislocated and torn between forgetting and remembering, and his characters are people like himself who reinvent themselves in a new city; but there still remains, "old selves, old traditions, erased in part but not fully. So what you get are these fragmented, multifaceted, multicultural selves." (Mavzorati, 44). After a while, the migrant does not remain a person who has moved from India or Pakistan to England; he is a man in general, who has no permanence, no stability, no sense of belonging anywhere. In fact, the migrant becomes a metaphor for the modern man who eternally drifts between two worlds. In *The Satanic Verses,* the set is that of London where the two middle-aged actors arrive after they survive a plane crash and meet more migrants like themselves; obviously it is a world of migrants. The character Chamcha is ill at ease in Bombay and in London because he is an outsider; his transformation into a goaty, horned and hoofed demon in the sanatorium is not to be taken as a physical transformation but as a psychological trauma. Another wording soul is Gibreal, lost in abracadabra of the absurd world:

> He floated over the parkland and cried out, frightening the birds.-No more of this England- induced ambiguities, clarity, clarity, at all costs, clarity. (353)

However, clarity is not the by-product of this absurd world because for an immigrant in the modern world, the psychological mutilation scams to be inevitable.

The Nowhere Man of Kamala Markandaya is the most suitable work to exlain the Diasporic instinct of the works of Diasporic writers; here she critiques an Indian immigrant's experience in Britain. She is an immigrant by choice and so can be grouped with Salman Rushdie, V.S. Naipaul N.C. Chaudhari and Ved Mehta, and share a common heritage and colonialism which bring the questions of identity in the Third World literature. In fact, Diaspora writers have one thing in common: that they evolve out of a dual cultural background, native and Western, and the common issue is that of the complication arising out of their immigrant condition; for instance, Salman Rushdie straddles two cultures and explains the emergence of a complex identity in *Midnight's Children*, and Hanif Kureishi in his film script *My Bautiful Laundrette* illustrates the cold reality of immigrant experience in England. Kamala Markandaya in her *The Nowhere Man* presents an immigrant's predicament in Britain over a period of 50 years, and reveals the effects of expatriation in him, bringing together alienation and loss which are nothing but the reminiscence of her own life, her colonial past and her immigrant present. No doubt the crux of the immigrant's dilemma is the question of identity, along with nostalgic yearning for the past and a sense of finality in exile. The immigrant loses his self-identity and does not belong anywhere, and he is a nowhere man, searching for a nowhere city. Anita Desai's character confronts a similar predicament in *Bye-Bye, Blackbird.* Anna Smith in her writings on Julia Kristeva says:

> The exile, the alien, the stronger, the eccentric are figures driven by unfulfilled desires and a lunging for love ... A similar marginality is to be found in the extreme psychic conditions and odd perceptual experience ... (17)

As Edward W. Said says in *Reflections on Exile:*

> ... exile is strangely compelling to think about but terrible to experience. It is the unhealab rift forced place, between a human being anf native place, between the self and its true home: its essential sadness can never be surmounted And while it is true that literature and history contain heroic, romantic, glorious, even triumphant episodes in an exile's life, these are no more than efforts meant to overcome the crippling sorrow of estrangement. The achievements of exile are permanently undermined by the loss of something left behind forever. (173)

Diaspora writing conveys a Diaspora experience which is a substantial record. K. Satchidanandan says in his article "That Third Space: Interrogating the Diasporic Paradigm":

> ... while one does not doubt the enduring value of the diasporic experience as a spring of organized inspiration, multiple identities, new subject sties, creative memories and fresh perspectives on language and life, a stage seems to have come when one should problematic the concept of the diaspora, no to deny to its authenticity as a state of experience but to quality, complexity and interrogate it in order to understand it better. (15)

No doubt, a Diasporic writer occupies a kind of second space, of exile and cultural solitude which Homi Bhabha calls a third space, a hybrid location of antagonism, perpetual tension and pregnant chaos in his *The Location of Culture*. K. Satchidanandan, further says:

> The reality of the body, a material production of one local culture, the abstraction of the mind, a cultural sub-text of a global experience provide the intertwining threads of the diasporic existence of a writer. (17)

Such Diasporic experience becomes a gendered experience when it comes to the writing of Indian woman abroad; and the minority majority status too contributes to the intensity of the felt alienations which is a bi-product of 'othering' experience within the Diaspora.

Precisely, the Diaspora writing is the writing of the writer who inhabits the third space, lives in the third culture and shapes the third history. Homi Bhabha is of the view that the discourse of the wandering peoples of the Diaspora marks a shifting boundary that alienates the frontiers of the modern nation. Obviously, it interrupts the monologic discourses of modern metropolises with their imperial memories; it challenges the monolith of the modern Western nation; and it may also foster cultural nationalism. In the same way, patriarchy, class structure and ethnic structure and ethnic conflicts can be reproduced and reinforced by Diasporic ideologies and its fabrications. K. Satchidanandan says:

> Destinations of class, sect and patriarchal norms within the family are also after reproduced by the diaspora as part of the reproduction of structures at home often viewed as the structures of the lost Golden part, and hence also of the promised future. Fortunately, more and more diasporic writers are becoming aware of the relativity of the concept of the diaspora, its inherent contradictions, with its multiple possibilities of alienation and assimilation, retreat into remembered patters and revolt against them, of being the colonizer and the colonized, marginal and the central. (20)

The arrival of the Diaspora writing into the world of Indian writing in English brought a sort of convulsion, rather, a sort of antagonism between the East and the West, between the cultures and between the identities, but finally everything was settled, a process of assimilation took place and now it has become an integral part of the bulk of Indian writing in English. Vijay Mishra in his paper titled 'The Diasporic Imaginary and the Indian Diaspora' defines it in a different way:

> All diasporas are unhappy, but every diaspora is unhappy in its own way. Diasporas refer to people who do not feel comfortable with their non-hyphenated identities as indicated on their passports. Diasporas are people who would want to explore the meaning of the hyphen, but perhaps not press the hyphen too far fear that this would lead to massive communal schizophrenia. They are precariously lodged with in an episteme of real or imagined displacements self imposed sense of exile; they are haunted by spectres, by ghosts arising from within that encourage irredentist or separatist movements. Diasporas are both celebrated and maligned. But we need to be a little cautions, a little wary of either position celebrating diasporas as the exemplary condition of late modernity—diasporas as highly democratic communities for whom domination and territory are not the preconditions of 'nationhood'—is not uncommon refrain. In the late modern celebratory argument on behalf of diasporas, diasporic communities are said to occupy a broader zone where the most vibrant kinds of interactions take place and where ethnicity and nation are kept separate. In this argument, diasporas are fluid, ideal, social formations, happy to live wherever there is an international airport and stand for a longer, much admired, historical process.

And all these factors go in the making of Diaspora writing. Shalem Singh in his paper tilled "Diaspora Literature—a Testimony of Realism' says:

> Diaspora literature involves an idea of homeland, a place from where the displacement occurs and narratives of harsh journeys undertaken on account of economic compulsion ... Diaspora writings are to some extent about

> the business of finding new Angles to enter reality ... The hybridity is subversive. It resists cultural authoritarianism and challenges official truths ... it forces, interrogates and challenges the authoritative voices of time.

Such writings are replete with the Diasporic consciousness which is nothing but the witness of all the happenings of social realities, longing and the feeling of belonging, for example, *Train to Pakistan, The Dark Dancer, Azadi, Ice Candy Man, A Bend in the Ganges, Twice Born, Midnight's Children, Sunlight on a Broken Column, Twice Dead, The Rope* and *Ashes and Petals,* etc. all depicting the woes and strifes of different kinds and different intensities.

Vijay Laxmi feels that an artist has to undergo some sort of 'inner exile' for creativity. However, real exiles have crossed national boundaries and by exchanging cultural codes have taken over the stage. They create an alternative world by exchanging tradition, culture, home and language. At the same time the opposition between the two cause anguish, existential dilemma of nothingness or not belonging. As Vijay Laxmi points out in her paper titled 'Of Immigrant Writing':

> The tension between what was and what is, between memory and reality, energizes the writer's work. The constant diving into the deep water's of memory help the writer reconstitutes or recreate a remembered part. In the process of recreation the writer evolves into a new being who is and is not the person who had started out. Memory, besides language, becomes the most significant factor that sets the diasporic writer's discourse in the centre ...memory, invented or real, helps the writer escape the confines of conformity and creates new literature a hybrid literature-which does not conform to any one tradition or culture, but creates a new world... . Inscribing two literatures, two languages and two traditions, the diasporic writers are no longer 'culturally homeless'. In their works 'the language of reverie... merges with 'the language of daylight life. (92-94)

So the Indian Diasporic writings with their initial nonentity entered the world of Indian writing in English, created upheavals and finally accepted/assimilated in its mainstream, now occupying a prominent position in text and meaning.

Works Cited

Abraham, P.A., *Crisis of Unbelonging,* in *Writers on the Indian Diaspora,* Ed. Jasbir Jain, New Delhi, Rawat Pub., 2007.

Ahmed Ajiz, *In Theory*, Bombay, OUP,1992.

Bhabha, Homi K., *The Location of Culture,* London: Routledge, 1994.

Bhattcharya, S., *Post-Colonial Literature,* New Delhi: Akansha Pub., 2004.

Gupta Ashis, *The Expatriate Composition of the Expatriate Writers,* in *Writers on the Indian Diaspora,* Ed. Jasbir Jain, New Delhi, Rawat Pub., 2007.

Laxmi, Vijay, *Of Immigrant Writing,* from *Dislocations and Multiculturalism,* Ed by Jasbir Jain, New Delhi: Rawat Pub. 2004.

Namloshi, Suniti, *Because of India,* London: Only Woman Press, 1989.

Parameshwaran, Uma, "*Home is Where Your Feet Are*", in *Writers on the Indian Diaspora,* Ed. Jasbir Jain, New Delhi, Rawat Pub., 2007.

Paranjape, M., Ed., *In Diaspora,* New Delhi: Indilogue Pub. 2001.

Prescott, L., *Past and Present Darkness: Sources of V.S. Naipaul's A Bend in the River*, Modern Fiction Studies, 30. No. 3 (Autumn 1984).

Rushdie, Salman, *A Dangerous Art Form*, Third World Book Review, 1, 1984.

____ *The Indian Writer in England,* in *The Eye of the Bachelor: Indian Writing in English* Ed., Maggie Butcher, London: Commonwealth Institute, 1983.

____ *Imaginary Homelands,* London: Ganta and Viking, 1991.

____ *Satanic Verses,* New York: Viking, 1989.

Safran, William, *Diaspora in Modern Societies: Myths of Homeland and Return,* Diaspora II, Spring 1991.

Said, Edward, *Identity, Authority and Freedom,* Transition 54, 1991.

____ *Reflections on Exile*, New Delhi: Penguine, 2001.

Singh, Gurubhagat, "*Expatriate Writing and the Problematic of Center*", in *Writers on the Indian Diaspora*, Ed. Jasbir Jain, New Delhi Rawat Pub., 2007.

Smith, Anna, *Readings on Exile and Estrangement,* London: Macmillan, 1996.

Index